YOUNG NIGGA$

THE NOVEL

OSACHAFO JAMAL BREWER

Archway Publishing books may be ordered through booksellers or by contacting:

Archway Publishing
1663 Liberty Drive
Bloomington, IN 47403
www.archwaypublishing.com
844-669-3957

ISBN: 978-1-6657-3580-3 (sc)
ISBN: 978-1-6657-3581-0 (e)

Library of Congress Control Number: 2022923804

Print information available on the last page.

Archway Publishing rev. date: 01/28/2023

For you Sach

INTRO

I never thought it would end like this. Coming from where I'm from they say the good die young and the older you become the more corrupt you become for your issue out of life. That issue could be anything; sex, drugs or alcohol whatever your pleasure. For me it was always something about the "paper" with the dead President's face on it. I had to have it by any means necessary. Whatever it took to get it I was with it. In the beginning none of us knew what selling your soul meant, but at the end of the day we were all caught up as Young Nigga$ ...

CHAPTER 1

I was born on the West Coast, raised in the beginning mainly by my Grandmother who was a prominent black educator throughout the bay area. Everyone knew Ms. Carter as a no nonsense teacher who was quick to put you in your place if needed but always going the extra mile for her students. Her in class tactics forced me to develop a good pair of hands and the nickname Scrap. She never knew I would have to defend her time after time. I would just make it home and let her put peroxide on my cuts. She would always finish with "Corey you're going to have to stop all this fighting." My only thoughts were as soon as you stop teaching I won't have to fight no more.

My Grandmother raised me and my two siblings in a middle class neighborhood. My older sister Goldie and my younger brother Lucki all shared a deep bond with our grandmother; each one unique in its own right. My brother being the youngest was the baby and that's what it was grandma's baby. My sister being the oldest and the only girl; well we will just say she got all the nice name brand stuff and me being in the middle I couldn't find a place to turn. So by the time middle school came around I was becoming a little too much to handle.

I can recall lying in a hospital bed with a fever of I don't even know how high but tubes were everywhere; all down my throat resulting from alcohol poisoning. I can still hear Gramma's voice.

"Corey you're going to have to pace yourself baby; you don't need to grow up too fast."

I realize now she was only speaking in my best interest but at the time it was falling on deaf ears.

Riverside elementary was the after hour hangout spot for me and my relatives. We would be there every day after school playing ball. At this time we all had hoop dreams of making it big in the NBA or some other professional sport. Kids from all over the city would meet up at Riverside and have pickup games for hours. It was always me and my relatives that made up our team. We were really family orientated and if you had a problem with one you had to deal with all of us. For that reason alone some people had long days but they brought that upon themselves. We were always seven strong. The eldest of us was Tone after him Fella and Lee; then me and Los. The youngest were Twannie and Joe. This particular day was just as normal as any other day. The courts were packed and we had just finished a game and were taking a water break. A few unfamiliar faces were hanging around watching the games along with some of the neighborhood D-boys. We had just run up and down against the Arabian team who were known to be physical because they were so uncoordinated. Every game they played was interesting because you never knew what would happen next. Say what you want about them, they weren't no pushovers. You couldn't be growing up in the bay allowing that, they gave as good as they got.

After making it to the water fountains for a quick drink we headed back to the court. The schoolyard had a big green dodge ball wall that stood between the water fountain and the court. Once we got on the backside of the wall I noticed everything about this normal day was about to change. One of the local D-boys who would come watch the games from time to time was standing with a pistol raised at one of the unfamiliar faces. He meant business and the look on his face showed it. He shouted, "didn't I say I was gon get you?"

Pop! Pop! Pop! Pop! I remember jumping in place where I stood then turning my back. I had never seen a body drop. I was so scared I probably cleared the fence with one step. To be honest I didn't even know if he hit the guy I just knew I did not need to be around to find out.

Unfortunately I had gone to this school the year prior to this happening and the fence I jumped happened to be in front of the cafeteria lady's house Pat or fat Pat as we usually called her. Well the shots brought her to her living room window only to recognize me jumping the fence in front of her house.

The police knocked on doors about the body that had been found on the school grounds. "Well! All I saw was Mrs. Carter's grandson Corey jumping the fence and running up the hill," Fat Pat said.

When the police pulled up to my Grandmother's they

nearly scared her half to death saying I was involved in a shooting and they would like to question me.

After I denied being at the school and said, "Ms. Pat (yeah I knew how to be respectful when my elders were in front of me) must've mistaken me for someone else."

I guess they figured they wasn't getting no answers from me. I was young and that was about the time Spice 1 was saying how snitches get stitches. When they pulled off my grandma just looked at me and shook her head. She knew I was barely going to school and I was out at all times of the night smoking weed and drinking. I think she had made her decision right then and there as the police backed out the driveway. She was sending me off to my mother who had just been released from prison out in Arizona. In her eyes she thought that would be the best for me.

Knowing I wouldn't want to go willingly, my grand-mother baited me with a pair of plane tickets to go visit my mother in Arizona. Using my relationship between me and my mother against me she knew I couldn't deny wanting to see her since it had been years that we were together. I can remember as clearly as yesterday when Grandma pulled up to my relatives house down the hill.

"Corey!" She shouted from behind the wheel of her min-ivan with my sister Goldie in the passenger seat. "Come here. I'm taking you to get a haircut so you can go visit your mama with Goldie in Arizona. You and your sister are going to spend some time with your Mama this summer."

It was the summer of '03. I had lived in Arizona before my mom had gone to prison but the memories had faded over the years. At that time my brother was off at summer camp. It didn't feel right leaving without him but the thought of seeing my mother was enough to go. I remember my girlfriend at the time was there at my relative's house when I pulled off with my grandmother. The last thing she said to me as I said goodbye to everybody was, "If you get in that car I ain't never going to see you again."

Thinking she was trippin, I pulled off and was on the way to the barber shop; then to go pack for my flight to Arizona.

CHAPTER 2

Arizona had felt as if we moved from the moisturizing sunshine to dry heat. I forgot about how hot it was. People looked at me and Goldie as if we were crazy because we had on jackets that were not needed at all.

What I had forgotten soon resurfaced when we pulled up to the house I remembered. It was a large step down from grandma's middle class. Now it was just trying to survive. It didn't bother us we were happy to be with our mom and it was only going to be for the summer. One memory that never faded was the Boys and Girls Club of America Holmes Tuttle branch. It sat right in the middle of the neighborhood. This is where I recalled having the most fun away from home. So after I unpacked and spent a little time with my mom I asked if I could go to the boys club. I had made it about three blocks away from my house before I was side tracked by a redbone female sitting on her porch. She was bad. She had a light skinned complexion with light red freckles and her hair pressed down to her shoulders. I had to approach her and me not being shy at all was not letting this opportunity slip by. I had to see if my game would work away from home. I called her to the gate to come and speak with me and asked her "how are you doing? My name is Corey."

"Hi Corey, they call me Rih."

"What you doing sitting out here? You look like you need some company." She laughed at my comment.

"Nah I'm straight, in fact my dad gon say something any minute now."

"Well that's too bad cuz I heard I keep good company." She smiled again and like clockwork her dad popped outside.

"Rih!" He called.

She rolled her eyes for me to see she wished he hadn't come out.

"Rih!" He called again.

"Look I gotta go but I'll see you around Corey."

"Alright then, I'll be lookin for you."

She turned and walked inside the house and as I watched her, her dad looked at me like he would break my neck if I ever gave him a reason to. I made my way to the club thinking I didn't even get her number then I realized we don't even have a phone.

The Boys and Girls Club was located on 36th Street. Walking up to the entrance I remembered some of the good times I had there and wondered if I would run into some of my old friends from the neighborhood. When I walked through the double doors I was all smiles; but soon after checking in at the front desk I felt the tension in the air from the cold stares from the other youngsters. Being familiar with confrontation I changed my smile to a mug instantly. I wasn't sure what the problem was but I was ready for whatever, whenever, however. That's when I met JBang. We were the same age and he eventually broke down all the politics to me in the neighborhood. Once he realized I was as green as Kermit the frog he explained to me why everyone had their mug on was because of the colors I wore. I now lived in gangland where the color of your outfit could mean a whole lot and it happened to be that day I was dressed like a rival when the actual fact was I was more like a foreign exchange student.

Gangs existed in the Bay Area but it was more of a Mexican thing. We were all family orientated within the Black communities. However, in Arizona I had to learn quickly where you lived meant a lot. The gang culture was everybody from the low to middle class Blacks, Mexicans and Whites that grew up amongst the minorities. This was the summer I was educated on the gangbang.

My neighborhood is Western Hills, located on the South central part of town. It is a fairly nice sized neighborhood that was patrolled and represented by three separate organizations, the Vista Bloods and the Vista Brown Prides which made up the Hispanic part of the neighborhood; and then the Western Hill Bloods which made up the Black part of the neighborhood. 36th street was the border and if you had no affiliation with any of the above named organizations you had no business around the area of Western Hill bloods or Pueblo Gardens. The Gardens was the neighborhood on the other side of 36th street. By the end of summer I was educated on this way of life.

My closest friends were Hawk, JBang, Vamp, and Studder. We had become like my family in the bay; if you messed with one you messed with all.

The day everything changed for me was at the end of the summer. I had made it home from the Boys and Girls Club only to see my sister had all her bags packed in the living room. It was about 2 1/2 weeks left of summer when Goldie hit me with the brutal truth.

"Scrap! Gramma only got one set of roundtrip tickets and that was for me; you'll be staying out here with Mama."

Right then it all unfolded like a cheap suit. I knew I was set up from the beginning and my girlfriend's words echoed in my head as Goldie began packing her bags into my mom's car. I know my grandma felt she was doing what was best for me but at the time all I felt was betrayed. Goldie was a part of that betrayal and because of that reason alone I didn't help her put her bags in the car nor did I ride with her and my mom to the airport.

After Goldie was gone I had to deal with the reality of addiction my mother had suffered with from the years before I was born. One noticeable and repetitive characteristic I peeped was that she would spend a significant amount of time in the bathroom. I would act as if I didn't notice but the truth was I did notice, in fact I noticed everything. The cold part of it was me, Vamp, Hawk, Studder and JBang were all going through the same thing; only my problem was in-house for the time being.

When the summer started I was the freshest kid on the block, the new kid from California. Now that school was starting I was as stale as a bag of potato chips that had been left open for about a week. My only option was to call my grandmother. In my eyes she was the one who had betrayed me. I learned early, pride will have you looking jacked up. I made my way to JBang's house because he had a phone

I could use. This was the call that opened my eyes to my situation. Either I would take control of it or I would fall victim to circumstance.

"Hey Goldie," I said when I heard my sister's voice.

"Corey, is that you?"

"Yeah it's me, how y'all doing out there?"

Before Goldie could answer my grandmother was talking.

"Corey, boy you must've known I was thinking about you. Are you alright?"

"I'm doing good gramma."

"That's good to hear Corey, you mind your mama now you hear me?"

"Yeah I hear you gramma, we're doing just fine too."

"Corey, did you get the money I sent you for school clothes?"

Right then my heart dropped into my stomach. "Yeah gramma I got it that's why I'm calling to thank you."

"Boy you know you don't have to thank me. You just listen to your mama and do well out there."

With that we said our goodbyes and hung up. The walk home was so frustrating. I was steaming like a tea kettle that was ready to be taken off the stove. All because I knew if the money was already sent, the money was already spent. When I walked through the door my mother was sitting on the couch. I slammed the door so hard the windows rattled.

"Boy what the fuck is wrong with you slamming my door like you crazy."

I instantly blew my top like a tea kettle, attacking my mothers' character about all that was bothering me. Then I finished by asking her how could she spend the money for my school clothes. My mother jumped up and went into her room. I swore she was going to get the belt to let me have it; but her door stayed shut and it was silent. It was like I was the parent disciplining my child for that moment and in that moment I realized if I wanted anything to change it was all on me. This was the hardest time for me; I was a grade behind and would have to borrow clothes from JBang early in the morning then Vamp and I would catch the yellow bus to school while JBang, Hawk and Studder all rode the city bus. I was in my head thinking while looking at Scrap gettin off the yellow bus. I hated it and couldn't wait till the next year to start high school. I knew I had to get myself together because high school was a whole different level.

The summer of '04 I would be turning 14 later in the year. All the youngsters would make their way to the Boys and Girls club; or to the park that was directly next to the club if the Director John had already kicked them out for the summer. Home was home. By this time my mother had moved in with her boyfriend and one of my older relatives lived at the house with me. My house was now a spot where the older members of the neighborhood hung out; ages ranging from 18 to 35. My relative was a known Western Hills Blood member that many loved to hang out with because it was no telling what would happen. My mother would come to the house from time to time and run everybody off but as soon as she left everybody was right back hanging out for a while. I just chilled at home because my house was where the party was at. But the fun was cut short that summer when my relative was locked up for attempted murder. After I had experienced the part of the neighborhood my relative had opened my eyes to, the park or the Boys and Girls Club wasn't all that appealing to me anymore. I had witnessed the fast dollar walk in and out of my yard and I wanted a piece of it. High school was about to start and I needed to come up and all I needed was the big homie Rock to feel my struggle.

CHAPTER 3

Rock was an OG in the hood who had for the most part a section of it on lock. He was known for showing love to the little homies so approaching him would be nothing. The other side of that is he was savage about his money. So although he was easy to talk to, he was the worst person to cross. The way I looked at it I had to do something. I was wearing my relatives hand-me-downs but that still wasn't gonna fly. So I made it my business before school started to catch Rock at the park. Bold and confident I said.

"Aye big homie"

"What cracking young blood?"

"Oh I'm mob-n you already know."

The big homie smiled, shook my hand and took a swallow of his Hennessy all in the same motion. Just as serious I leaned in and said.

"Blood I need to make a move. You know it's all bad since they put the clamps on the big relative. I got all this traffic stoppin by the house and can't do nothing with it."

After I explained my situation in detail to Rock he knew

he could capitalize on another spot in the hood and all he had to do was supply the product. My mom had small traffic coming through and the ones that didn't know my relative was locked up were still stopping by.

Rock gave me a chirp line to call and told me to meet him at my house in 20 minutes. I'm in motion, this was actually happening. On my way towards my house JBang caught me crossing 36th Street, he said.

"What's good my nigga!"

"Awe it ain't shit what it do"?

"What was you and the big homie talking bout? I saw ya'll chop'n it up."

"Awe shit he was just asking me about the relative; was he good and shit like that."

"What! You ain't coming to the club?"

JBang gave me his sideways look when something wasn't quite right.

"Naw my nigga I'm finna head to the crib and post up. I'll get with you in a minute."

"Alright Blood b's Scrap".

"B's my nigga."

With that we shook hands and walked in separate directions. I looked back to see JBang walking into the Boys and Girls club. I thought to myself I ain't trying to walk through them doors for the rest of the summer. JBang was my nigga but he loved to bullshit and joke around. As bad as I wanted to tell him what I had going on with big homie I couldn't, JBang would've told everybody and the shit would have been canceled before it even started. I could not risk that no matter how bad I felt for not telling him.

Forty five minutes after I talked with Rock he pulled up

in front of my house in his 1966 Impala Super Sport con-
vertible. I hopped in the passenger seat and Rock placed
a brown paper bag in my lap and said.

"Look lil nigga you said you wanna make moves so
make moves then. Playtime is over; therefore it's no reason
for me to see you at the park."

I shook my head in agreement. Rock then let me know I
had an $1,800 debt over my head. It was crazy that I felt no
stress about it when in all reality it was hard to get 8 dollars
let alone 1,800 of them. Before I got out of the car Rock said.

"Chirp me on the line I gave you when you ready. It's a
chirp in the bag just for that."

I hopped out but not before Rock let me know I was
playing with the big boys. My mom stood in the doorway
as Rock pulled off. She just shook her head as I walked into
the house with the brown bag in hand. She already knew
it was too late. In my room I emptied the contents of the
bag onto my mattress. It contained a box of razor blades,
a box of sandwich bags, a digital scale and most importantly 4 ½ ounces of crack cocaine. I stared at the dope in
amazement to the point where I started daydreaming on
making it big and how much money I had to make before I
was free of debt and on my own shit so I made a chart and
called it Operation Blast Off. I had to see it on paper. Unit:
36 zips = 72 splits=144 midgets= 288 babys= 1008 gs,
Estimated Price Range $18,500 - $22,000, Targeted Price
Range $18,500 Gross $23,040, Net Profit $4,540.00

½ Unit: 18 zips = 36 splits = 72 midgets = 144 babys
= 504 gs, Estimated Price Range $8,500.00- $10,000.00,
Targeted Price Range $9,000.00, Gross $11,520.00, Net
Profit $2,520.00.

¼ Unit: 9 zips = 18 splits = 36 midgets = 72 babys = 252 gs, Estimated Price Range $4,000.00 - $5,500.00, Targeted Price Range $4,500.00, Gross $5,760.00, Net Profit $1,260.00

4 ½ Zips: 9 splits = 18 midgets = 36 babys = 126 gs, Estimated Price Range $1,800.00 - $2,200.00, Targeted Price Range $2,200.00, Gross $2,880.00, Net Profit $680.00.

2 ¼ Zips: 5 splits = 9 midgets = 18 babys = 63 gs, Estimated Price Range $900.00 - $1,200.00, Targeted Price Range $1,000.00, Gross $1,440.00, Net Profit $440.00.

Now I know I only had 4 ½ zips and my net profit would be around $2800.00 after I paid Rock off. These numbers made my thoughts about having an Impala like Rocks real and having money, clothes and everything that came with it. The feeling of making it to the top from the bottom was what consumed me. When I snapped out of it I went into the kitchen to grab a plate. I had watched my older relative chop dope enough times so I knew the sizes of each piece. So when I made it back to my room I locked the door and grabbed one ounce. I then found a stash spot behind the drywall in my closet where I hoped my mom wouldn't find it and I placed the 3 ½ ounces in it. I pushed the button to the digital scale to turn the power on. Then I put the scale on gram mode and placed the ounce on it; it read 296. This was some serious shit going on; I knew I had to be accurate in order for me to avoid any problems. I took the ounce and opened the plastic it came in and set it on the plate. Grabbed the razor and applied pressure to the dope until it snapped. I repeated this process until the ounce was chopped. I swear I felt richer every time I heard the snap. I calculated $1,000 from my fat pieces that no one could complain about the quantity or quality. That was part of the game though; to complain when they were actually jonesin trying to get another hit. After everything was put away I walked out into the living room to see one of my mom's friends sitting on the couch. It was a neighborhood smoker named Lil Nicki. While my mom was in the bathroom I used the time to run my campaign.

"Aye Lil Nicki whats good?"

"Awe Scrap baby what's up?"

"Awe I got work for the workers."

His eyes lit up as I placed two of my boulders in his hand.

"That's you right there but you make sure you bring that money this way."

Lil Nicki jumped to his feet and said. "Awe Scrap you ain't said nothing, you done made my day." With that he was gone and it was just a waiting game. The other spots shut down early in the hood and everyone else was curb servin so I made sure I let Lil Nicki know I was open all night just knock on my window when it got late. The wait wasn't long at all. 15 minutes later Lil Nicki was back. "I got sixty Lil daddy." I handed him his work and he was gone again. I remember sitting in my room holding on to that sixty like a nigga that never had nothing. It's a different flavor when the money is going in your pocket. That night the money kept coming. I ended up passing out with six hundred in my pocket and by the next afternoon my first oz. was gone.

I repeated the same process with the rest of the work. When it was all gone I calculated $4100. That was the most money I had seen at that point in my life. Thoughts ran across my head like: I could buy my own plane ticket now; but the reality was I wasn't making no money back home. The seed was planted and after each transaction it grew stronger. I was home now. That was when I learned a valuable lesson, as I day dreamed, about what I could do. I looked in awe at the money. Then I heard Lil Nicki at my door yelling, "Scrap! Scrap!" I stashed my cash then opened the door. "What's up Lil Nicki? Why you yelling like somebody chasing you?" He laughed it off and came in my room.

"I got a hun-ned lil daddy. Bless me like you did the last time."

"Awe Lil Nicki you gon have to wait. I'm out right now. Give me a hot minute to get right again."

With that Lil Nicki looked as if I spoke Chinese to him and was out the door too damn fast for me. That's when I learned in this game you always had to have the product for the customer or the customer would go somewhere else. I chirped Rock with the number he gave me and he chirped back.

"What's good little nigga?"

"Awe it ain't shit I need you to pull up on me with the same thang."

"Oh you ready for me? He asked."

"Hell yeah I'm ready. I can't wait all day though."

Rock busted up laughing through the speaker. "Alright, alright young blood, give me 20 minutes."

"Alright big homie"! With that I hung up and counted out $3600. My plan was to pay what I owed and purchase my own sack. I wasn't with owing anybody. When Rock pulled up he didn't even look surprised when I handed him the $3600. He just said "I knew you was a muthafucken hustler," then handed me another 4½ oz in a brown paper bag.

CHAPTER 4

I hustled hard for the last 8 weeks of the summer and when school started my hard work showed. The house was lightly remodeled with new carpet, couches and bedroom sets for me and my mom with an entertainment system in the living room. My mom was even dealing with her addiction a lot better. The feeling was unexplainable things were actually getting better. When I look back all I wanted was some gear to go to school and ended up obtaining a lot more. My prize possession and pride and joy was my white on white 1984 Cadillac Coupe Deville. It sat on 22 inch Dayton wire wheels and had a system out of this world. All you could hear when I pulled up was David Banner's Cadillac on 22's I ain't did nothing in my life but stayed true. I couldn't even leave the neighborhood because I didn't have a license but everyone knew whose car it was thanks to Rock, that's who I bought it from.

My freshman year started and I didn't need no more bus passes after all. This was a moment in my life I will never forget because I was truly happy. My house was getting better, my mother was getting her stuff together and I had my own car and my own hustle. My mom's girlfriends would say, "Scrap that's a grown man's car." Without being mannish as my mama would tell me not to be, my reply was simple. "Not if that grown man don't hustle." My summer job proved hustling was all I did and by the middle of the school year I was up to 18 ounces in my stash and 12K in my mattress. Nothing was fronted it was all mine. It had looked like an overnight success story to some because my once struggling household now showed the signs of a livable residence. I would see some of the older homies pass by looking but not saying much. When I had enough of the cold stares I called Rock to explain the situation and learned a valuable lesson.

"Aye my nigga it's time to let yo niggas eat in this game. First you get the money, then you get the power but to keep it all you gon need the muscle."

I was getting money and the power the money brought. I wasn't blind to it but for the same reason them older niggas was passing by was the same reason Rock explained it was time to put my niggas on. In a community where money defines everything especially if you are successful, some-one else is losing. It's like knocking food off your neighbor's plate. My success had a few niggas meals getting short and that reason alone had them checking out the competition. It was now time to boss up. Rock instructed me to give all my hand to hand sales to my Nigga$. At first I didn't understand why I would give up all the clientele I built then Rock ex-plained to me selling wholesale was where the real money is even though I was only taking in $550 an oz. from the usual $900 to $1000. Rock said "the faster you flip the more you stack." Then it all became clear since I would have JBang, Vamp, Hawk and Studder all grabbing their work from me.

CHAPTER 5

I was becoming Rock's young protégé. Everyone in the hood knew it and wished they had the position I held. I'm sure a few were jealous but couldn't show their cards because they knew how Rock felt about me. The money we made changed a lot of niggas over time. In the early days I made sure I brought it to the light when someone was acting shady or funnystyle towards my Nigga$. During that school year we was the Nigga$. I was just a freshman but I moved like a senior. I would be at school by 8:00am and gone by 1:00pm. The classroom was just a place where I talked to the honeys and thought about all the money I was missing back in the hood. The teachers for the most part were just as uninterested as I, talking about some shit that wasn't relevant at the time. Rock even encouraged me to stay in school but the first year of high school ended up being my last. We all had dropped out to become scholars on the blacktop. If I could go back I would finish school but we live and learn. I can go back even further by acknowledging we should have paid attention to the words on the paper that said In God We Trust but it was too late we had been bitten by the money bug.

Trap'n came easy to JBang, Vamp, Studder and Hawk. They would play catch in the street with the football and take turns making sales. It was a non-stop hustle and the police paid us no attention. I can honestly say it was easy because the dope basically sold itself; all you had to do was to have quality product and make it available. By the middle of the summer we all was on 24hr all-nighters which paid off in big ways. Hawk purchased a Coupe Cadillac like mine and sat it on 20 inch Daytons with the Vogue tires. It was two toned burgundy and white, JBang had a 86 Regal limited black on black with chrome 20 inch Dayton spokes, Vamp who was the youngest of us had to have those 20's on his box Chevy Caprice painted money green with peanut butter leather and Studder rolled his steel gray Cutlass Supreme that sat on 22's and had pipes and a motor out of this world. We sat the hood on fire every time we pulled off my block. Everybody was looking, they had no choice we was shining.

The older homies all did their thing on a block called Coconino. They hustled all day on the block and wore Cincinnati Reds hats to represent Coconino. No Young Nigga$ hung out over there; that was for the Y.G.'s and O.G.'s that were active all around the board. A lot of shit happened on that street. It was at that time the heart of the hood. Since we wasn't allowed to really be on Coconino unless it was for business purposes, like us needing to buy some weed or something; we decided to come up with our own click and style for our block. We knew everyone referred to us as them young niggas. It was then we started wearing New York Yankee hats for the N and Y and we flipped it to the Young Nigga$. At that time we were only five super swagged out youngsters who never knew how we would eventually end up influencing every young brother in the neighborhood. We were just having fun but ended up starting a movement; everyone wanted to be like us with their Yankee caps on. Due to the hood fame of the Young Nigga$ the cash flow on Coconino was getting slower and slower each day. That reason alone frustrated a few people on Coconino. The main one who did not appreciate the new entrepreneurs was known in the neighborhood as Face. His gun tactics and the work his boys put in on Coconino was for the main supplier Ricky Slick.

Ricky Slick was known as a boss in hood. He rarely made appearances but when he did you knew he was around. All I knew was Slick and Rock was the big dogs in the hood. To me Rock was more accessible because he was always around. We realized later that we were too young to notice let alone understand the politics of the hood and that a turf war was brewing between Rock and Slick. The dawning came when we found out whoever supplied your block would be the side you were on. All of us being young thought that since we was all from the same hood that it was all good. I'll never forget the day Rock said. "How long are you gonna be good with your neighbor knocking your food off your plate?"

CHAPTER 6

The summer we all got on was the summer everything changed. We were posted on the block. Studder and I sat on the porch while JBang and Hawk stood in the street tossing the football to Vamp until he got tired and left them to it. My block ended at a park parking lot so basically it was a dead end. Whoever came in we saw them leave the same way. As JBang and Hawk continued playing catch we heard the sound of tires screeching then saw Face turning the corner in his bubble Caprice. When he saw Hawk and JBang in the street he floored the pedal and the motor rev'd up loudly picking up speed. JBang and Hawk rushed to the curb barely making it before they were hit. Driving crazy was normal in the hood but this nigga here was on some other shit. Hawk shouted, "What the fuck up wit that nigga Scrap he almost hit me"? Face was deliberately trying to mow them down. As Face circled in the parking lot he paused his Caprice once he was facing to come back down the block. He hit the brake then punched the gas at the same time causing his rear tires to spin and burn rubber. He eventually released off the brake pulling out at high speed he fired shots in the air as he passed my house. Pop!pop!pop!pop!pop!pop! "Oh that nigga on one my nigga," Vamp stated. We watched him ride down the block then make that left onto Coconino disappearing into the neighborhood. I didn't know what was up with that nigga but I was gon find out. I went inside my room and chirped the homie.

"Aye big homie, this nigga Face just set it off on the block right now."

"What happen? Rock asked."

"The nigga damn near ran the homie over in the street then he slid back by poppin off in the air."

"Is that right? Listen! Scrap I want you to meet me at the spot in the Gardens."

"Alright big homie I got everybody wit me too; be there in 15 minutes." With that I hung up and went to let my Nigga$ know we was go meet with the big homie. Once we pulled off the block and headed to the Gardens I could feel it in the air that something big was about to happen. I just didn't know what it was. Hawk chose to leave his whip at my house and ride wit me. I think he was feeling the same but he never said so. The spot in the Gardens was less than 5 minutes away so we were there before Rock pulled up. When he did he said "follow me inside Scrap." Everyone else waited in the yard until we came out. I had been to this spot before to pick up packages from Rock but that was always done in the driveway; I had never been inside. Walking in I thought this is why I had never been inside. The living room was bare as if no one lived there. No furniture, no nothing. From the outside it looked like a livable decent house. The Gardens was a better looking neighborhood than Western

Hills from the outside looking in; but in reality both sides were still the ghetto. "Lock that door." Rock stated as I locked the door and followed him down a hallway that led to the backroom where Rock fumbled through his keys to unlock about five different locks. I asked Rock.

"What's all the locks for big homie?" Rock looked at me and said "you just remember you don't tell nobody what you've seen behind this door." I nodded my head in agreement but not before Rock made sure I understood by saying

"I mean it, don't even tell them Nigga$ outside what all you seen behind this door."

"Alright Big Blood I got you."

With that he opened the door and told me another valuable lesson.

"Young Scrap never let niggas see how you coming or where you coming from. You see how I only let you in. I know them your Nigga$, but you my nigga. Always keep niggas guessing young nigga."

Walking in I understood why he had all the locks to the door plus the bars on the house that made it look so secure. The room had gun racks along all the walls from the floor to the ceiling with enough guns to supply a small army on some rebel shit.

"So you said it was Face right?"

"Yeah big homie, that's who it was, I don't know why he tripped out like that but he wasn't tryna be on the low either."

"Ricky Slick must've told that nigga to shake ya'll up; here grab them 5 Rugers and 2 A.R's right there."

"What's these Ruger nine's?" I asked.

"Yeah, blood grab them shells for the Choppa's in the closet and I got some shells for the Rugers in the kitchen."

"Alright big homie."

As I grabbed the shells for the Choppas my churp went off. It was my mom. "Whats up mama?"

"Scrap these niggas done shot my house up."

"What?"

"I said these."

"No mama I heard you, you alright?"

"Yeah baby I'm fine, but hold on the police are pulling up right now I gotta go, I'll call you back."

She hung up so quick I didn't get any information. I was in complete denial. I went into the kitchen and told Rock.

"Rock them niggas done shot up my crib."

Rock paused for a second then said. "This is what I want you to do. Take what I'm giving you to this address on the eastside. Her name is Chocolate and she already know what's up. I'll call her when we leave here. He wrote on a piece of paper then said everybody get a nine and you hold them Chops for the crib but don't go home till you hear from me; alright homie Imma take this call then I'm gone."

With that I grabbed an army surplus bag that was in the kitchen and placed the Chops in it along with the Rugers and shells for both. When we walked outside I opened my trunk and sat the bag behind my speaker box. Vamp stated.

"Aye my Nigga$ when y'all walked inside it sounded like someone was getting off in the hood."

"I already know my Nigga$ they hit the block up." "What? Vamp asked. They shot yo Mama house up?" "Yeah blood it's bad right now. She say them people all over there."

Hawk, Studder and JBang was in disbelief. Just like I was when I heard but Vamp was heated.

"Them bitch ass niggas! That's how they want to play it? Alright alright watch just watch."

"Calm down my Nigga$ don't even trip. We gonna go lay low for now. Here y'all take these." I reached in the surplus bag and handed each one a Ruger and a box of shells. They're eyes lit up like Christmas but Vamp had another look, a sinister one, once I placed a gun and bullets in his hand.

"Y'all Nigga$ follow me to the east, the Big Homie go get at us in a minute."

Everyone agreed but I could tell Vamp wasn't feeling it. Vamp being the youngest plus the livewire of the click wanted to retaliate. Before we hopped in the cars and pulled off Vamp said. "Them niggas are goin to think we some sucka soft punks." He was the only one loading his clip while I explained our next move. Rock came out the house and looked at me and said,

"Why you still here you already know the script?"

"Alright blood we gone" I replied.

We pulled off and out of Pueblo Gardens and Vamp was the first to break formation. He turned right into the hood; I knew exactly where he was going and it was too late to stop him. Hawk looked at me and said "you already know what he on."

Pullin up to the East side residence I parked in the driveway while Studder and JBang parked on the street. As soon as I bounced out the Cadi I heard the high loud pitched voice of a woman and a door slamming behind it. "Aww hell naw boy you park that on the street." This girl was bad, chocolate skin tone with the body of a goddess and her lips were as juicy as a fresh strawberry. I had to pop something slick at her real quick. "Wait a minute baby! I'll move it but when I beep beep you go open up so I can pull in?" She stormed off stomping her feet but not before I jumped back in and hit the horn. Beep beep! JBang was the first to complain. "Damn Scrap you just had to say something." Next thing you know the garage door popped open. Slowly I looked at JBang with my crooked smile that said don't ever doubt me, I got this.

CHAPTER 7

Her name was appropriately Chocolate. She stood in the doorway in all her fineness looking like a million in my head; I had to have her. I pulled the Cadi in the open two car space next to a Civic, never breaking eye contact. I let my eyes show I wanted to tear that ass up and she knew it because after I hopped out she said. "Just as mannish as you wanna be." Then she turned and walked into the house. After proper introductions my concerns went to Vamp. I chirped him but got nothing leaving me to think I hope this Nigga$ didn't do nothing stupid. When Vamp broke formation he had one thing on his mind especially when he made a right on Norton Vista. Knowing he would probably make another right on Cochise Vista bringing him right where he wanted to be on Coconino Vista. He rolled his window down creeping up the block. After passing the first set of speed bumps he could see the Coconino block was active because of the low riders lining both sides of the street. Idling slow down the block Vamp gripped his Ruger tightly as he inched closer. From the porch Face spotted the Caprice creeping

but was too late to call it. Coconino was packed with gangsters waiting on the next sale. Vamp put Cisco in his sights
taking aim. Pop!pop!pop!pop!pop!pop!pop!pop! Vamp fired
and Face returned shots right back. pop!pop!pop!pop!po
p!pop!pop!pop! dropping Vamps rear window before he
made the left on Forgeus and was out of sight. When Face
turned around Cisco laid on his back gasping heavily and
Worm laid stretched out yelling "I'm hit! I'm hit! I'm hit!"
The damage was on Cisco; he was struck twice in his upper
torso and pronounced dead on arrival. Vamp headed to his
girlfriends on the eastside at the Mayfair Manor apartments.
Walking inside he finally decided to chirp me back. "What's
good my Nigga$?"

"Oh it ain't shit" he replied."

"Why you break off formation?" I asked.

"Awe shit I had to handle something."

"My Nigga$ pull up on me I'm on Golf Links and Pantano.

"Shit I'm outta commission right now my whip is all bad."

"Catch a cab then my Nigga$."

"Alright give me a little bit, I just got over Stephanie's I'll
be over there though."

I gave Vamp the address and hung up. When he pulled
up to Chocolate's we were in the living room watching vid-
eos. Chocolate let him in and we all went to the backyard
to hear what had went down. "Before you trip Scrap let me
tell you straight up. I know we was supposed to head over
here but I'm gon keep it 100 blood. I wasn't feeling that shit
my Nigga$. We in the hood, we can't be going out like no
pussy boi's you feel me! I had to hold it down for the block."

"I know my Nigga$ but the big homie wanted us to come
over here before anything else went down" I replied.

"I got somebody though; I know it should be bad for at least one of them niggas." Vamp stated my whip is all fucked up. I got my shit parked at Stephanie's. It's probably hot anyway now."

After we were all filled in we went back in the house. We all knew what time it was now. It was what we called in the hood Funk Season conflict. Wasn't nothing in the hood we wasn't use to but we were usually in the hand to hand combat type against cross towers; now it was hood to hood and gunplay involved. This was some shit that would either make us or break us. I thought about all types of shit to myself like were we ready for what laid ahead for us. JBang was the joker, he was the comedian type of the click always on some funny shit that would have you cracking up, Studder he was the chubby lover boy always tryna please the ladies and whenever his girl called he was ghost but that was our Nigga$ regardless cause we would push for him with no hesitation. Hawk was quiet, like myself more obstinate than anything else; he was always about what benefited all of us and not just about himself. We had a thing that we always knew what the other was thinking or when someone was on some bullshit. Then it was Vamp, the youngest but also craziest of us all. He didn't have his gun for twenty minutes before he pulled off and clapped somebody; but no matter what we was squad, The Young Nigga$.

CHAPTER 8

My thoughts were interrupted by my chirp, it was Rock. I walked into Chocolates' room to talk since she was in the master bathroom taking a shower. "What's good big homie"?

"Y'all over there posted" he asked.

"Yeah big homie we all here."

"Where Vamp at?" This intentionally got my nerves going. I was thinking aw hell why did he ask that? I said as nonchalantly as possible, "shit he right here, what's good?"

"I'll be over there in a minute don't even trip."

I hung up with that question in the front of my head and went and pulled Vamp to the side. "Aye my Nigga$ that was Rock; he was asking about you. What you want to tell him?"

"Man fuck it Scrap, it is what it is; we go give him the uncut version when he pull up." We shook hands and that was that. I don't know why I was so rattled about Rock asking about Vamp, hell Vamp didn't even give a damn. I realized then that I never heard back from my Mom. So much had been going on that it damn near slipped my mind. I went back to Chocolate's room and called from my chirp. The first call I got no answer, as I attempted to call the third time Chocolate came from the bathroom with a towel wrapped around her body and another one around her head looking as soft as a feather stuffed pillow. Hello! Hello! H e l l o! My Mom was screaming into the receiver snapping me out of my daze.

"Mama!"

"What Scrap?" She replied somewhat annoyed.

"Mama! You alright over there?"

"I was until you woke me up; boy are you okay?

"Yeah Mama I'm good."

"Good! Now what do you want?"

"What did the police say?"

"Oh they were trying to search the house but I heard on their radio the judge wouldn't clear the warrant because I was the victim so I closed the door and went to bed."

"So everything's good Mama?"

"Yeah Cory everything is alright baby, but they did take Hawk's car when they noticed it had bullet holes in it."

"What!"

"I said they took."

"No I heard you Mama; I'll be home in a minute, sorry I woke you up." My Mom knew when I said a minute that could be a minute to a few days. I was blessed that the police weren't allowed to search my house. My whole life was in that drywall, it definitely would've been a whole different story had a warrant been granted. All I could say to myself was at least my stash was safe.

Chocolate reached in her nightstand and pulled out a box and sat at the foot of the bed. In the box she started breaking down the weed it held and twisted a blunt. When she finished she scooted closer to where I sat and placed the freshly rolled blunt between my lips then put flame to the end of it. As I inhaled then exhaled the large cloud of smoke I thought to myself this is my kind of bitch. By this point I had my way with all the hoodrats. I had even got Rih to sneak out the house a few times but Chocolate was on a whole different level. She was older, had her own crib and car and did her own thing. I just hoped she wasn't big homie Rocks' wife because the mutual flirtation had begun on sight so I had no choice but to ask. "Aye whats up wit you and Rock?"

"What do you mean?" She asked in a soft tone."

"Don't play you know exactly what I'm saying; is that yo nigga or something?" She busted up laughing then replied. "If he is, I'm hella outta pocket; I've known Jason for a long time. He looks out for me from time to time and I sell pills for him in the club. I'm a dancer at the Candystore. So to answer your question no we ain't together or nothing like that." We sat on the bed smoking and getting to know each other. She told me how she had been in a few abusive relationships with some fucked up niggas and how she was a loyal bitch but niggas always found a way to do her wrong. That left the door swinging wide open for me to walk in. "Aye baby, don't judge me by your past mistakes. I need a loyal bitch down with the ship I'm on. Once you see a contradiction on what I say or do then tell yourself you can't do it no more because I'm sure I won't contradict nothing if you as real and loyal as you claim to be."

She smiled and said. "All I can do is show you." We hit it off instantly; she wasn't even concerned about my age.

She was 20 and I was about to be 15 but my hustle had me 25 mentally; so I thought. I had it all put together like a masterpiece art collection.

Chocolate told me she had to go to work and wanted to know if we would be there when she got off. I wasn't sure so I gave her my chirp line and told her I would leave the key under the flower pot in the backyard if we left. Once she was dressed I walked her to her car in the garage. "Alright I'll be off at two. I hope you'll be here but if not I'll chirp you once I get home." She kissed me on the cheek, hopped in and pulled off. As soon as I walked back into the house JBang got silly "ooh wee Scrap done knocked that bitch, you better hope that ain't Rock's bitch."

"I already asked so its all good; that nigga ain't finna get on me behind some pussy." Everybody busted up laughing. We were restless as we sat in the living room and it seemed time was not our friend the waiting was making us anxious. Studder asked. "Damn Scrap when the homie going to pull up?" "I don't know my NIgga$ but he said he would be here. I knew Studder just wanted to get to his girl. If he wasn't on the block he was with her. Rock didn't pull up until midnight. He walked in the house wearing all black like he just got off a mission. "Alright my Nigga$! Its all bad in the hood right now. The police got shit hotter than fish grease. Vamp! Whats up blood? I told you to come straight here for a reason."

"I know big homie but I."

Rock cut him off in mid sentence. "Where that Ruger at lil nigga? Vamp reached into his waistline and pulled out the Ruger and handed it to Rock. Rock smiled and grabbed young Vamp huggin him in excitement. "Boy you knocked that nigga down; you just got your first body."

Vamp just simply asked "who was it?"

"That nigga Cisco dead and you hit Worm in his thigh but he'll make it." We were all surprised to hear what we heard from Rock. I think we just thought he popped a nigga but he terminated one and popped the other. Rock reached in his waistline and handed Vamp a 40. cal. "that's clean Young Nigga$, I'll get you some more shells when we get back to the hood." The first sign of emotion Vamp showed was when Rock placed the 40. Caliber in his hand; his smirk was just as sinister as the devil himself. All JBang could say was "Aye big homie let me get a 40. Cal."

Rock simply and coldly said. "Knock something down and you'll get one." We all busted up but JBang wasn't feeling us. Rock let me know to chill at Chocolate's until he chirped me and with that he was gone.

We ended up drinking and smoking slamming shot after shot. I sat back and Cisco came to mind. I knew it was real now, then I glanced over at Vamp and he moved like it was just a regular day with no care in the world. His eyes locked on mine and simply said. "Aye Scrap fuck that nigga it is what it is. We the Young Nigga$!" Right then I knew Vamp was a damn nut. They all passed out before Chocolate came home, but Vamp and I were the last ones up. I don't even know if he went to sleep, but what woke me up was the sound of the shower running. I glanced at the clock and it was 3:20 am. When Chocolate came out of the bathroom she looked as good as she did earlier. She asked me, "did I wake you?"

"Yeah something like that but I was barely asleep though."

"Yeah right it looks like y'all had a party. Everybody was knocked out when I came in." She then asked. "You tryna smoke wit me?"

"Twist it up baby." She smiled then repeated the same process from earlier rolling then placing the blunt between my lips. I lay back inhaling the tree and watching her as she caressed her skin with an oil that smelled good enough to arouse a dead man. I grabbed the remote to distract myself and began flipping through the channels trying to find something on late night. "Oh yeah I almost forgot." Chocolate bounced up off the bed and hurried to the bathroom. When she came back she held her clutch bag in her hand. As she fumbled through it I laid back as if I wasn't paying her no mind. She pulled her stack of ones out and it looked real healthy. She said. "It was kind of slow tonight for most of the bitches but I did my thang." Handing me her stack she said. "This is for you, now you in control so don't fuck me over Scrap." I pulled her soft body close to mine and told her. "Don't you worry bout a thang baby I got you." Chocolate had handed me $1,100 dollars. All I could do is smile while she rested her head on my chest. The total emotion I felt had to be contained because she kept looking her big brown eyes right at me. I kept it real player; "colder than a blizzard in Alaska '' as Mac Dre would say.

That night we talked until the sun cracked the morning sky. When I finally woke up it was after twelve but I could smell eggs, bacon, sausage being fried and biscuits baking. Pretty sure those smells just might be what woke me up. I stepped out of Chocolate's room and walked right into JBang jokes. He whispered to me "you must've put it down; you got her making breakfast for the FAM." I just shook my head and walked past him directly to Chocolate and grabbed her from behind kissing her on her neck. "Damn baby you made me pancakes too I see you."

"Yeah babe I just thought you would be hungry when you got up." She replied. Chocolate was a natural beauty looking all early morning sexy. She really didn't need no makeup but she could work the hell out of some lip gloss though. We all ate and by five Chocolate was out the door and on her way to work. Again we were restless and waiting to get back to the block. It seemed like Rock had dropped us; my churp was silent. The only reason I was content was because I had Chocolate every night breaking me off in numerous ways. I think she was trying to pussy whoop the Young Nigga$. We ended up staying 5 days at Chocolate's before we got the chirp from Rock. I thought the homie had forgotten about us. "Aye Blood, y'all get back to the block and hold it down. You already know if you gotta bang then bang my Nigga$."

"Alright big homie."

CHAPTER 9

Now the time had come to see who was really built for this. There was no turning back. I had Chocolate follow me to the hood just so she could see the block and grab a few outfits to take to her house so my presence was always there since she had already made me a key. Vamp and Hawk rode with me because the police were still investigating and holding his Cadi but he had his Aunt trying to get it daily. When we pulled into the hood Vamp clutched his 40. Caliber as if it was about to go down. We passed block after block and every Young Nigga$ who was outside saluted our caravan. Chocolate witnessed it all from behind when we pulled up to the house. Hawk grabbed the AR's out the trunk while Chocolate followed me in the house where my Mom sat on the couch. The first thing she said was "Scrap I can't have all that nonsense going on where I lay my head. Niggas shooting and not caring who that bullet hits. Police all around the house trying to run up in here." I had to cut her off or it would've never stopped.

"Mama ain't nobody going to do nothing like that again

I promise you." I really had no clue what would happen. All I knew was I would be here to prevent it.

"Hell they were shooting last night on Coconino so I don't know how you expect me to believe that." I knew this was a fight I couldn't win so I just introduced her to Chocolate and then walked into my room. It made no sense to give her false hope. She knew better than that. Once she said it had gone down just last night it wasn't no telling what would be happening.

After Chocolate grabbed a few of my items she followed me back to the porch where Rih was sitting with Hawk, Vamp and Studder. She was saying "Yeah niggas got hit up real bad last night on Coconino; they say Danger and Loon got knocked off." We all looked at each other with no reply for her but we knew if that was the case it was getting really real around our parts of town. Loon and Danger was part of Ricky Slicks inner circle of goons; they just wasn't no average niggas.

Chocolate stood on the porch holding my Jordan gym bag of clothes looking at Rih like bitch why are you over here? She then walked the bag to her passenger seat then purposefully walked straight to me and kissed me on the cheek and said. "Alright daddy I'm gonna go get ready for work so we can get this money." She glanced at Rih again like a broke bitch, walked to her Civic and pulled off. Rih had it all on her face how she wished we had something more than our little fling but that's how it was in the hood; she was the home girl and that would never change.

Once Rih was gone Vamp was like "Damn it's been going down. Danger and Loon! "My Nigga$ you know they go try to strike some shit." We posted all night, the money started flowing and we watched for the retaliation but the only thing that came was the money. I sensed we all wanted to prove ourselves like Vamp did and that's probably why nothing happened that night. Whoever planned on pulling on our block wasn't gonna make it off.

The next few days it was the same routine. We were back and the hood was quiet for the most part. We did get the word that Ricky Slick had put a $20,000 price on Rocks head for what happened to Loon and Danger. When Rock got word of it he was officially on some other shit. He wasn't hiding, he made sure that point was known but he wasn't flashy either anymore. He would pull up in his low profile car or underbucket as we called them, then he'd bounce out amp'd up to the max with bullet proof vest, pistol in hand and looking everybody directly in their eyes. Sometimes I wondered if he thought I was go bust his ass. Homie was paranoid but showed he wasn't going nowhere. When we would be alone he would then let his guard down and say. "Remember you can't never let these niggas see where you coming from Blood, especially when niggas putting prices on heads. Most of these niggas can't stack 5 grand so what you think they go do for 20g's? Scrap my days are numbered now; but to eat we still gotta hustle my Nigga$; you remember that." When Rock pulled off I thought to myself ain't nobody fuck'n wit the big homie. The next time we linked up was 2 days later early in the morning, he was on the hunt for some cheap work. "Aye Scrap you still got work?" he asked.

"Yeah I'm good right now big homie, its still go be a couple days before I re-up."

"Well shit I'm going to pull up on you. I need you to hold this package while I handle something on deuce nine."

"Alright Blood I'm at the house." Fifteen minutes he was at my door with a Louie duffle bag that had four birds in it. I'll be back to get this in a little while.

"I'm to meet up wit lil Mumu right now on the Eastside; he got the plug on more work for the low."

"Alright big homie chirp me when you on your way." With that Rock jumped back in his Ford Taurus and was gone.

CHAPTER 10

Mumu was a fast talking hustler who looked to the middle man for anything he got his hands on. He wasn't from the neighborhood but he was connected to it. He knew he could get Rock to bite on the cheap price because they sometimes dealt with the same plug who was taxing them both. When Rock hopped in the Taurus the plot was set.

"What's good Mumu?"

"Awe it ain't shit maine, tryna get this money what you been into? Mumu asked."

"Oh you know I'm play'n Uncle Scrooge in the ghetto. "What's up with this work is it good?" Rock asked.

"Maine you know I ain't go have you cop no bullshit. This Mexican got ran off from the Westside so now he on the Eastside tryna find new clientele. I already copped a chicken and cooked it; it came back beautiful baby."

"Awe shit here you go."

"Nah Rock for real maine you know I fucks wit you. I cooked it by the 9 and it blew to 13. I know you tryna fuck wit that."

"Hell yeah I'm tryna fuck wit that where he at?"

Greed is something you will always have to manage in this game or it will lead you right to your own destruction. Mumu led Rock through the heart of the Eastside where anybody from Bloods, Crips, gangsters and Mexicans could pull up on you and leave you right there. "Say maine pull up to the market next to the Las Casitas, I met him right there last time. I'm go run inside real quick and chirp him, you want something?"

"Nah I'm straight just hurry up shit." While Mumu was inside he chirped Face, who was sitting in a stolen van in the Las Casitas apartment complex directly across the street with another shooter, who went by the name Bone. Rock sat behind the wheel of the Taurus in front of the market as the mini-van pulled on the side of him and slid the door open. Flacka flacka flacka flacka flames from the Mac90 chopper ripped through the Ford Taurus like Swiss cheese. Flacka flacka flacka flacka more shots find their target slumping Rock over his steering wheel causing him to sound off his horn. Over 30 rounds ripped through the Taurus before the van pulled off and out of site. Mumu had stayed around to answer all the necessary questions. "I just ran in the market to grab a drink and heard all the shots; when I came out my man was dead." The power move was made and the O.G. was down. If I knew that would be my last time to see him when he dropped off the duffle bag; I would have thanked him for being a real Nigga$ and lacing me to the game. Greed was what really got Rock in the end, it was fatal. Ricky Slick would now be pushing his chess pieces forward. He wanted the hood and figured nothing and no one was in his way any longer.

Rock's funeral was one like the Southside had never seen. I had met with his wife for the first time days before and arranged for the Young Nigga$ to be the pallbearers. Bosses and gangsters from all sides of town showed up to pay their respect to our neighborhood legend. The Young Nigga$ all wore white dickie suits that were air brushed with Rocks face on the back and wearing our Young Nigga$ hats. Our shoes were white, Air Force 1's that were also air-brushed with R.I.P. on one and Rock on the other. Everyone had brought out the cars as we were all sitting up in traffic. After the burial it was like a celebration as we swang the rides from left to right leaving the Southlawn Cemetery. I think people just joined the caravan and came back to the block because, to the average person in traffic it looked as if we were headed to a party. When we got to the block I sat on the porch looking at all the people throwing up their hands and giving it up for Rock and I was like damn my nigga was gone and wasn't no changing that.

Chocolate must've felt my vibe because when she came out of the house she looked at me and then walked over to me twisting my hat to the back and sitting on my lap, placing her arms around my neck she said. "Daddy I know you fucked up about it, but you gonna have to snap out of it and see whats in front of you. Look at all these niggas celebrating for Rock out here and thats yo nigga and everybody here knows that. As soon as you open your eyes to it you go see it for what its worth; this is what he left you baby." She kissed me on the cheek then rose and went back in the house with my Mom. I had always known she was a real bitch but she had just motivated me as to what I was to become. That moment I called my Nigga$ to the porch and told them it was our time. They looked at me knowing I was about to take them to another level; then I gave them all the game to boss up like it was given to me by Rock. They scouted the packed street like lions looking at their cubs. All the young niggas out there may not have been ready for what we were about to do but we didn't miss the ones that were. When the night was over Vamp, Studder, Hawk and JBang all had 7 youngsters a piece. It was crazy; it went from four local Young Nigga$ to adding 28 young and hungry workers. Now the pressure was on me to make it all happen.

The next couple of days I turned corners in the hood finding houses for rent. I had Chocolate get at a few of her girls from the Club who needed to make an extra buck or two to put houses in their names. Two weeks after Rocks funeral I had all the houses ready for the takeover. On Coconino niggas was out having a good time because they felt the nigga who caused all their problems was out their way. Little did they know it was a Young Nigga$ who looked at it different.

CHAPTER 11

Ricky Slick had told a few of his goons to ride around the blocks telling everybody it would be a meeting at the park that called for the Original Gangsters, the Young Gangsters, and the Baby Gangsters to be there. At this time we were considered BG's, the baby gangsters in the hood; but our click was the Young Nigga$ and we wasn't attending. I did have a few of the new recruits go and spy on what was said but none of the original Young Nigga$ from my block was there. Hawk had us calling him ill Fetti, who came back to let us know what was up. "Yeah big bro this nigga was like, we all from the same hood, the same soil. There ain't go be no more hood on hood shit pop'n off over here. He said if anybody get outta line he go see to it personally that it get dealt with; then the nigga went on to say if you selling work in the hood it better be hood dope and all the hood dope is coming off Coconino. So if you ain't pull'n up on Coconino and cop'n your package it ain't coming from me and that's going to be a problem straight up. He also said the beef between the young and older homies is squashed, if we play'n to win that shit must cease to exist. This is the Hills and we set the standard of the town so we go do this shit right." I had heard enough and my Nigga$ had too. Ricky Slick was really feeling himself and it made me wonder what had been said behind closed doors when he realized none of my Nigga$ was there.

The houses were located on Cameron Vista, Norton Vista, Sunland and Cochise Vista. All these blocks surrounded Coconino in some type of way. Any smoker who wanted to get high and go to Coconino would have to pass an active block of Young Nigga$. The way I looked at it was if we made it slow with one block we were about to shut it down. Hawk had Cameron Vista, Vamp had Cochise Vista, Studder and his squad was on Sunland and JBang was on Norton. I knew when the blocks got really pumping we was gonna catch the flow of traffic coming from South Park, another neighborhood one city block west of us.

I had Chocolate on the hunt for a connect. She had kept coming up short because the people she was introducing me to were small-time and not ready to deal with what I was tryna do. The frustration was building because I had to come up with something fast. I had a lot invested, from security deposits, to just the dream of the Young Nigga$ holding the hood down. If it wasn't for the package that Rock had left none of what I already did would have been possible.

Rock had left me 4 birds and I had 2, that gave me 6 when he passed, but now that I opened up 4 blocks I was down to 1 with no connect yet and it was serious out there.

The blocks were buzz'n and that 1 could be gone by the end of the week. The homie had been gone for about four months and we had the hood on fire. Smokers were coming all the way from across town because the Young Nigga$ had love for them. Big stupid rocks they called it. When Face reported back to Ricky Slick he was pissed off. "Man homie the block is slow as fuck and these Young Nigga$ is everywhere. They got Cameron, they got Cochise, Sunland and Norton. I swear I'm ready to wake some shit up around here." Ricky Slick sat in silence long enough that Face had to make sure he was still on the phone. Then he asked. "Who they cop'n from Face?" "They must be get'n that shit from Scrap," he replied.

"You mean to tell me Young Scrap is feeding four blocks?"

"That's exactly what I'm saying." This pissed Slick off. "So Rock put him on like that huh." He laughed to himself; then Face asked.

"What you want me to do Slick, start knocking these little niggas off?"

"Naw give him a little more time his supply should be getting low by now. He'll be coming your way, he just don't know it yet."

CHAPTER 12

November of 2004 I was turning 15 and we was all on the block in front of my Mom's house. Chocolate was excited, she wouldn't stop calling because she planned on getting with me and my Nigga$ in the club. She had set it up through the bouncer but I really wasn't feeling it. I had heard all the stories about when Chocolate would get off. To me it sounded like a bunch of niggas spending money they didn't have to spend. Frontin for the females was a crime where me and my Nigga$ came from. The Young Nigga$ wasn't into giving money away we was into making it.

I was down to 9 oz's it was bad in my eyes. I didn't know what I was going to do and it seemed all Chocolate cared about was me coming to the Club. She chirped me again. "Whats up Daddy when ya'll coming?"

"I don't know yet you got something poppin I asked." "Why you acting like that its yo birthday daddy."

"I don't give a damn I need a plug baby."

"See you always fucking up your surprises."

"So what you saying Chocolate?"

"I met this Mexican who done spent a lot of money on me and I told him about you; he seems like he's about his business and I told him you would be coming in. He said "we'll see what happens.""

"Just cause he tricking don't mean shit baby."

"I know daddy but he Gucci, Louie, Polo." That was our code for saying he was on his shit.

"Alright, give me a minute we will be up there." With that I hung up thinking to myself if her job was to sale me a dream to get up there she did that. I told Hawk, Studder, JBang and Vamp we was about to step out in a major way and hit the Candy Store. All the other Young Nigga$ went back to their block and grinded. After we all left and got dressed we met back up. JBang was already amp'd. "I'm finna be on them bitches watch." We all knew he was go show up and show out. When Chocolate called again we were leaving the hood. By this time we was all riding again. Hawk had got his Cadi back from the police impound and Vamp was back in is box Chevy. "I'm on my way" I said through the churp. Chocolate was so excited because all the shit she had been telling her friends at the Club was about to have a truth to it. We was all fresh like the produce section in your local supermarket but we liked to use the term Sliced.

We pulled up to the Candystore in Western Hills fashion. The paint on every vehicle looking like a jolly rancher; finding our parking spaces I chirped Chocolate. "I'm out here." We all bounced out and all the bitches in the line looked at us like a filet mignon tastes. It was crazy because the bitches smiled but the niggas frowned. Chocolate came out and escorted us past the line to the bouncer at the door.

"Bobby this is Scrap and his Boys; the ones I was telling you about."

"Oh ok Chocolate! The bouncer held his hand out and greeted me. Happy Birthday! I shook his hand then reached in my pocket and pulled out a large fold of money and tip'd him a C-note; from that moment on we was V.I.P. Soon as we walked through the doors JBang lost it. "Young Nigga$ in the building." He shouted as he tossed a stack of ones in the air. Chocolate had reserved a V.I.P. table for me and my Nigga$ on the balcony overlooking the stage. We were the center of attention and my Nigga$ was showing the spectators how to really ball out. The bottles came and the party was where we were. Chocolate had already changed into her street clothes so she could live it up with the Young Nigga$. The DJ had got on the mic. "I wanna send a special shout out to the man sitting up in the balcony Happy Birthday Scrap." The scene was live and my Nigga$ cashed out hundreds for dollar bills then rained on the crowd from above. Everybody there wished they were in V.I.P. that night; we had it pop'n. Chocolate sat next to me enjoying the night; but all that was on my mind was the "Connect" she had talked about. All her friends made their rounds introducing themselves. Even the females she didn't like came up to say hi. Chocolate was having a hell of a time because her stories had truth to them. She would brag to her home girls that she was fuck'n wit a young nigga who was doing more than most of the niggas that come in this club that had age on them. But like I said it was only one thing on my mind.

"What's up with the plug?" I asked her.

"He's downstairs daddy." She replied.

"Well what good is that gonna do me?"

"What, you want me to go and get him now!"

"Nah Chocolate I want you to sit here and look pretty all night." She knew I was getting irritated so she bounced up and said. "Alright damn I'm going." I slapped her ass real hard as she walked off. She liked that and looked back at me and smiled as she made her way downstairs. She really didn't want to let me out of her site because the thirsty hoes were all over the place. It wasn't my fault she had told all them stories about me. If she kept her mouth shut we would've been just some average niggas in the club. As soon as Chocolate was out of site a sexy ass bright skinned female sat down next to me. She had long wavy hair and looked like something out a video. She was jazzy and thick too. She had those eyes when you made contact with them it was hard to look away. She was drip'n with sex appeal and she knew it. "Whats up Scrap?" she asked.

"How do you know who I am?" I asked and she smiled and said.

"You'd probably be surprised what I know about you." My eyebrows raised at that and I said.

"Is that right!"

"Yeah that's right." Right away I thought to myself this one right here is feisty and fine.

"Ok then since you know my name it's only fair you tell me yours."

"They call me "Diamond."

Chocolate was coming back up the stairs so Diamond slid me a napkin and whispered in my ear and said "here's my number. When you ready to come get yo present for your birthday, call me." She stood up and walked off just as Chocolate was approaching. Chocolate looked her up and down then back at me and asked. "What that bitch want"? She had the Mexican standing right next to her and she was about to get on some bullshit. "I know you heard me Scrap what was that bitch doing up here." One of Chocolate's friends pulled her to the side while the Mexican stood looking somewhat awkward so I had to take matters into my own hands since Chocolate was way off the script. I stood up and extended my hand to the Mexican. "How are you doing, I'm Scrap." He shook my hand and I directed him to sit next to me. I offered to buy him a drink and signaled for the waitress to come over. I pulled out a large bankroll so he could see I was about my money. I could tell from his attire he was about his; all the while remembering what Rock had once said to me "the only thing that money was attracted to was more of it."

CHAPTER 13

Flaco was his name, he looked about twenty-five, but he carried himself as a seasoned vet.

"So Chocolate says you're looking for a connect" he asked.

"Yeah that's right." I replied.

"What happened to your last one?"

"Well shit he got killed a few months ago so I'm kinda stuck right now with my supply getting low. Flaco watched the whole scene and vibe of everyone. My Nigga$ was enjoying themselves tossing money in the air like tomorrow wasn't coming. "What are you prepared to cop right now?" he asked.

"Shit it don't matter what you have"? I then realized I was talking to the man, because in the past when I said whatever you got the dealer Chocolate had introduced me to would say something small like a half a bird or a nine pack. Flaco had the look of a business man and the polite cockiness that said there's no way you can cop all of what I can supply. "I can grab four bricks right now but I bet you wanna take it slow since we just met so I'll grab two from you to see how it goes." He shook his head as if he was doing numbers in his mind then he asked. "How old are you Scrap"? I had almost lied but then I thought about it. I was doing what that 20 year old should be or what that 25 year old could be doing so I said "shit man today is my birthday I'm fifteen."

"Fifteen! Flaco responded in disbelief. Its your birthday?"

"Yeah man." I replied. Then it all made sense to him. Why my Nigga$ were showing out, tossing money and pop'n bottles. He told me. "Scrap, I like you; I got a feeling about you. You're real reserved. Here's my number, call me tomorrow and we can do some business together." We shook hands and Flaco made his way back downstairs. I had the waitress send a bottle to his table to show my gratitude for the opportunity that was presented.

Chocolate sat back down after Flaco left with her arm crossed and lips poked out. She was still upset about the Diamond situation. "My girl told me that bitch was on you as soon as I walked off; she's lucky I don't shut this bitch down and hit her ass with a bottle across her head."

"Awe baby come here." I broke the tension she was giving off and put my tongue on her ear and her mood changed instantly. "There's the smile I'm looking for." I said teasing her.

"You play'n, stop daddy I'm serious." I knew she just wanted my attention and I planned on giving it to her for the rest of the night. She had found the plug I was looking for; the connect that would keep the bricks alive and pump'n. We continued having a good night and it was about time to wrap it up and take it to the block. A few of Chocolates' home girls were choose'n on my Young Nigga$ and making their way downstairs. Vamp had wandered off downstairs, then made his way back and pulled me to the side and said. "That nigga Mumu downstairs." We had never got the chance to catch up with Mumu after what happened with Rock and he didn't show up to the funeral which only added more suspicion. I walked over to the balcony to catch a glimpse of him and Vamp pointed him out. Once we made eye contact I signaled for him to come join us in VIP. "What's good with it Young Scrap? Y'all up here living it up too." I had to hold my mouth tighter than frog pussy when Mumu said that shit; but of course Vamp had not yet acquired the simplicity of just being silent for a moment so he started whistling the theme song of America's Most Wanted, What cha go do when they come for you. Oh Mumu caught it alright but let it slide on by changing the temperature asking "how y'all get in?"

"Oh shit I was plugged in, you know how we do." I replied, trying to disguise my feelings as much as possible. "Yeah, you know its my birthday. I had to do it big one time. My thoughts were this nigga probably lying but my mouth said. "Is that right! I didn't even know.

"That's why all the bitches up here? What y'all into after this?"

"Shit we got a few bitches coming to the block you tryna fuck wit us?

"Hell yeah! You know I am, I gots to fuck wit my Young Nigga$ tonight; shit it's your birthday Scrap. With that I sat back, had a few more drinks while watching this nigga perform until I was ready to bounce. I told Chocolate to meet me on the block with her homegirls. I told her we had to leave before the liquor store closed so we could have something to drink.

Everybody said their temporary goodbyes then bounced out. Once we got in the parking lot we noticed Mumu hoping into a GS Lexus that was known to be Ricky Slicks. Vamp barely sounded civil when he asked Mumu. "That's you right there Mumu?"

"Yeah maine I had to park the Regal and get on my grown man ya dig."

"Shit that look like Slicks Lex"

"It is. He made an offer I couldn't refuse; I had to snatch it up."

"That's whats up, well shit we finna go get this alcohol follow us."

"Alright maine."

I hopped in my Cadi steaming. I couldn't think straight about shit. This nigga had his nerve. Ricky Slick was known for paying niggas cars for bodies. The niggas who just wanted to stunt was his main customers and Mumu was a prime candidate. When we pulled onto Hawks block instead of mine I assumed my Nigga$ knew what time it was. We parked and bounced out. "Yeah maine if y'all need that work get at me I'm on right now." Mumu bragged. After about 15 minutes of small talk Mumu had become impatient. "What's up with them hoes Scrap?" "Shit my nigga you know they take a hot second to pay everybody and get out of there, they'll be pulling up." When I looked at my Nigga$ I saw it in their face they were all hungry. "Say maine I got some of this kill I'm go twist up. It's that purple shit and this shit is no joke."

"Shit what you wait'n fo burn that shit." Vamp stated.

Mumu sat in his Lexus and started twisting a blunt; we all looked at each other like the perfect opportunity had presented itself and enclosed on Mumu while he sat in the Lexus like a pack of lions on a gazelle. Pop! Pop! Pop! Pop! Pop! Pop! Pop! Shots from our Rugers and Vamps 40.cal found their target as he attempted to roll a blunt. Pop! Pop! Pop! Pop! Pop! More shots ripped through the Lexus leaving Mumu slumped over the middle console. Over 30 rounds were fired but you could never tell because the block was quiet as a library. We pulled off and headed to my mom's. Chocolate sat on the porch with her homegirls as we pulled into the driveway and when I got out Chocolate said. "Daddy I just heard hella shots right now."

"Oh yeah! I couldn't hear shit wit them gorilla's in my trunk tryna get out" I replied. Her friends started laughing and all she could say was "you so silly."

That night we posted until the wee hours of the morning. It took that long before we heard the ambulance. We all knew they were too late. Once me and Chocolate went inside everyone else went and got a room. I didn't expect to hear from my Nigga$ for a few hours. It was a long night.

The next afternoon I was awakened by a cold splash. "What the fuck!" I shouted as I realized Chocolate had dumped a bucket of ice water on me while I slept. She stood at the edge of the bed, eyes teary with the look that she had been hurt deep.

"How could you Scrap?" She asked.

"Man, what the hell you talking about?" I was still in shock pushing all the ice cubes out my bed. "I been down wit you Scrap I can't believe you. I still had no clue what she was on. "Baby I don't know what you talk'n bout; you trip'n."

I rose to get out of bed and she said "you know what I'm talking about and threw a napkin at my chest that fell to the floor. Right then I knew exactly what it was. I had slipped up but I had to twist it in some type of way. Chocolate what you doin going through my shit? It didn't help in any type of way. Chocolate looked at me with the coldest stare she had ever gave me up until that point in our relationship; she then turned her back walking away saying I'm doing laundry but in the calmest and softest tone possible. Yeah it spooked me and I said to myself "this bitch is crazy." She was boiling inside but reserved her anger because we was at my Mom's house. I knew I had a lot of making up to do. I thought how did I let her find that number and out of all the numbers to find it was Diamonds.

CHAPTER 14

It was around 3:00 pm when I called Flaco. Hello! He answered. "Whats up, this Flaco?" I asked." Yeah who's this he replied." "This is Scrap from last night at the Candy Store." "Aww yeah Scrap whats up my friend."

"Shit I'm ready when you are."

"Ok how long will it take to get to Midvale?"

"Shit I can be there in 30. Is that cool?"

"Cool! Go to Walmart and call me when you get there."

"Alright I'm go grab two."

"That's all good; call me when you're close." With that I hung up and counted out the twelve grand that we had agreed upon at the club. Rock was charging me sixteen grand. I was now at 12.5 a kilo. I was excited because I knew I was winning. As I counted the money out Chocolate sat on the edge of the bed painting her toenails. She said "I told you that was "the connect." I placed the money in the duffle bag and kissed her cheek saying "yeah baby you did that now come on we taking yo car."

On the ride to Midvale all Chocolate did was complain

about her car. I knew she was hinting that she wanted a new car. She deserved one for making this deal happen but she was going to have to wait so I told her. "Baby let me flip this pack a few times then I'm going to have you in something tight." She smiled and said "ok daddy." For a while it was like the Diamond incident had left her mind. She got off the freeway on Valencia and I made the call. "Yeah I'm getting off the freeway now."

"Ok Scrap I'm already here; I'm at the east entrance in the 3rd lane; look for a yellow Dodge Ram pickup with black racing stripes. It's a Rumble bee, you know what that is?" "Aww yeah I'll find it, I'll be right there. I hung up and directed Chocolate where to go. Moments later I was in the 3rd lane looking for a space to park. I had found a spot about two cars over from Flaco's pickup. Once Chocolate parked I grabbed the duffle bag off the floorboard and hopped out the Honda. I instantly noticed two Hispanic men in a truck directly behind from where I was parked. I started walking towards Flaco's pickup and spotted another truck with two Hispanic men parked right behind Flaco. I made it to Flaco's truck and hopped in the passenger seat where Flaco was sitting alone, but I couldn't help but to notice lined right across from us backed in was the 3rd truck facing us also with two Hispanic men sitting inside. I now knew I was slipping with 25 grand on me and it was too late to turn back. "What's good Flaco?"

"Aww you know man just enjoying this day" he replied." I handed him the duffle where he ran his fingers through the money until he was satisfied. "That's twenty-five right there" I stated as I watched the two Hispanic men across from me. I knew it was another two parked behind me and two more that could jam Chocolate up in the matter of seconds but I kept my cool. Flaco nodded his head at my statement then reached into his middle console then pulled out two bricks that were wrapped and stamped with the Louis Vuitton logo. I asked Flaco if he had a knife; he smiled and said "you know I do" then pointed to the glove box. I couldn't keep my eyes from looking at the men in the truck across from me because they were watching me like flies on shit. I grabbed the knife and cut both bricks enough for me to stick the tip in and taste the coke and took a quick snort up my nostril. With that done I knew I had the real deal and some really big thangs was being initiated if I walked away intact. I coughed and knocked off any powder left on my nose. Flaco asked "Es bueno right?"

"Yeah it's good." I replied. Thinking to myself I still had to walk out of this situation so I brought up what I was feeling. "Aye man next time just me and you do the deal; no more trucks alright?" Flaco looked at me and smiled like he was somewhat surprised that I brought it up; but it wasn't like it was hard to notice. "Ok man you know this was just the first time you gotta be careful out here." I shook my head in agreement and I was starting to feel the effects of the coke so it felt like I was shaking my head hella fast. "Yeah man next time you can come to the house and meet the fam, it's all good." He agreed and we shook hands then I placed the work in my duffle as Flaco placed the money in his console. Walking back to the Honda I swore one of the Mexicans was gonna rob me for the package. The coke had me paranoid to the 10th power. I had let my excitement of finding a connect override the chance I was taking. It could have been a set up with the police or a straight out robbery for the money. All the good business that spoiled me with Rock had me walk into a situation like everybody was good when I know better. I had put Chocolate and myself in a fucked up situation; but I did learn from it. Chocolate instantly knew something bothered me when I got back in the Honda but I couldn't tell her. "What's wrong daddy?" she asked. "Nothing, just drive." I replied.

Back in the hood I broke the packages open then cooked the powder 9 ounces at a time blowing it up to 12 and a quarter ounces. In this game it was explained to me by Rock that if I wanted to win I would have to learn to cook. I learned it all from Hick watching him place the powder in a jar, add the baking soda then turn it into crack using a slow cook and very little water. The powder would break down to a jelly form then with the turn of the wrist you became a chef. I ended up learning different techniques but I was now on the Pyrex blender whip'n. We lived in a community where some chef's survived just off the cook. If you tell him its 9 ounces then that's what you'll get; all the extras was his or in some cases hers. We called that free coke.

The blocks was pumping pack after pack. The Young Nigga$ was out and active on every corner I turned. All I saw was Yankee hats basically and I can't lie this was a beautiful time. Airbrushed Yankee shirts were everywhere. It showed that the Young Nigga$ was here. By this time I had flipped the pack from Flaco a few times and the blocks were consistent. The Coconino boys were frustrated and ready to shut down; mainly it was Face but Ricky Slick felt as if it was nothing he couldn't control, to him all we were was Young Nigga$. His moves were strategic and Face was the exact opposite. He would kill just to make a point even if the point made no sense; but right now he had to follow orders.

"Damn Slick these little niggas still got work and Coconino ain't seen a dollar in days."

"You know what Face you right, something does gotta give. Them little niggas fuck'n with my money now; and they was foul for how they left Mumu. I was willing to overlook that disrespectful act but now they trying my patience." "Is it Scrap? He asked."

"Hell yeah its Scrap; its Scrap, Vamp, Hawk, Studder and JBang. Who you want done first?" Face asked as he clutched his weapon ready for the answer."

"Naw naw just bring Scrap to me, I guess Rock taught him more than I expected. It's time we have our face to face. Don't touch him like that, just bring him to me. It's time we put a little pressure on this young boy." With that Face hung up the phone and shook his head looking at his ace Bone. "Let's go snatch this little nigga up."

I sat at the house watching the game through the brief interruptions from Chocolate. "Daddy you gonna go get the hot links?"

"Yeah I'm going to wait till half time."

"The steak is about to be done, you need to go now." I could smell the steaks and here them sizzle, the buttered corn boiled and the pork aroma from the greens was busting into the atmosphere. "Alright I'm going." Studder was chirping me for another pack so I had to make a run. It was Sunday afternoon in the hood my mom was at church. She had found Jesus and was getting herself together. She once made her money cooking dope which supported her habit and somehow she was able to make the choice of not wanting to be around it. The people who she once let come around wasn't allowed to no more. Lil Niki had even stop coming over. Everything was looking like a good day. The Young Nigga$ saluted as I passed through the blocks. When I pulled up to the market I bounced out my Cadi and caught JimJam out front asking for change. "What's up JimJam?"

"Awe Scrap shit gimme a couple dollars."

"I'll do you a better one what you want?"

"I just told ya shit gimme a couple dollars." "I laughed and reached in my pocket and handed him some singles." "Alright Unk you be easy maine." Walking in the market it was just a regular day in the hood. I grabbed the links from the meat man and had my Arab bro put a bottle of the Remy in the bag. In the ghetto good days turn bad within a blink of the eye and as soon as I felt the afternoon sun stepping out of the market my day was about to get a whole lot worse. Bag in hand I noticed Face and Bone on the side of the container that held block and cubed ice clutching their weapons. I was slippin all the way; my weapon sat on the floorboard of the Cadi under the seat. It was no way I would make it to it; and the looks Bone and Face had let me know they meant business. They must've read my thoughts of wondering if I could make it to my Cadi because Face said "go ahead and I'm go lay yo ass down right here." Bone looked like the Grinch not saying a word just ready to terminate. They walked up on me and I had to keep my cool. All I could do is try to get the attention of people going in or coming out the market. "Man what the fuck y'all want?" I tried to speak loud but the people who did notice what was going on acted like they didn't. That's just how it was in the hood. "Don't get loud nigga, walk yo bitch ass over here." They snatched me up like a play toy for pit bulls walking me to the side of the market. I noticed Big Dirty behind the wheel of a Tahoe. The backup came and I was tossed in where Bone had me at gunpoint while Face zip tied my hands and feet and placed a dark pillow case over my head. They joked and even laughed as we pulled off. Face said "this nigga was slipping for real fam." "What desert we go leave him in?" Bone asked. "We going to the west let them vultures eat on his ass." They all laughed at that and I knew it was over; all I was waiting for was the bang! Then my intellect kicked in and I thought, why would they blind fold me if they were going to kill me? Either way it would be a ride that I'd never forget. Every time I tried to move from my lying position I was punched in the ribs. I realized there was no escaping this shit.

The ride seemed like an eternity. I flashed back to my innocent days and right back to what was all coming to an end. I was no longer innocent. Rock's words kept pop'n in my head; it was the day he gave me my first package. He said, "You play'n with the big boys now, Scrap." Soon I'd hear the car coming to a final stop then it would be over. Instead I heard an electric garage door opening; it closed after we eased in a few more yards. I heard Face and his crew slam the doors then pop the back where I lay tied up like a calf at a rodeo show. I was snatched up and forced to walk blindfolded; I couldn't see shit through the pillow case. I must've been triple bagged and tagged for the slaughter when the bag came off. I saw Face's devilish smirk then he pushed me in a room that was boarded from the inside to the outside. The door slammed and I heard as many locks click as Rock had in his gun room. This room had a surveillance camera watching my every move; other than that it was bare, no carpet, no furniture no nothing. I leaned against the wall and slid down until I hit the floor thinking to myself it's a wrap but wondering why I wasn't dead yet.

CHAPTER 15

Back in the hood Chocolate was going crazy. She had called everybody telling them I was just going to the market then coming back to eat. Everyone pulled up to my moms and then Vamp and Hawk rode to the market to see if they saw something. When they got back they had a look that indicated something was wrong. Vamp said. "Scrap Cadi is at the market but he ain't nowhere in sight."

"What! Chocolate shouted, do you mean his car is up there?" They got him y'all I'm telling you they got him."

"Calm down Chocolate, he's probably handling some business real quick." Vamp stated.

"I'm telling y'all something ain't right I can feel it."

JBang, Vamp and Studder all tried to chirp Scrap but got nothing. Hawk tried to keep Chocolate from going hysterical but it wasn't working. My chirp sat in my console while I sat in a cold ass room. I knew my Nigga$ were looking for me by now. I sat in the room until the small glimpses of sun stopped showing through the small cracks of the plywood. Then the locks were being unlatched from the other side of the door. Bone stood there looking at me like dog chow. He said "get yo punk ass up." He had a pistol in hand; all I could do is comply. My thoughts were if I make it outta here his days will be numbered. Bone led me down a hallway that led to a dimly lit dining area actually more like a den where three men sat at a Cherrywood knights table. Two of the men I was more familiar with than the one who was sitting in the throne chair of the table. Face and Dirty sat next to him looking at me like they had a problem I was born in this world. Bone directed me to sit at a chair that was available. He then took a few steps back but kept his pistol on me.

"So this is young Scrap, the mastermind behind the madness in my hood. You know who I am?" The voice in the throne chair asked." I knew exactly who it was now. It was Ricky Slick and he thought and believed everything was his. "Yeah I know who you are."

"Then you must know that you are in violation and that it's going to be up to you if you want to live or die today." I sat quiet because I knew the wrong remark would have me in the desert. I knew this was Ricky Slick and he would work his angle if I let him but Bone, Dirty and Face were just waiting for the order to off me. "You see Scrap I'm a businessman and before any more blood is lost, I'm willing to overlook what you did or had done to Mumu. You see the hood is like a machine and I got all the parts to it. This machine has a Patent that makes anyone who tries to duplicate it in direct violation and that's where I am at with you. You created a machine that already exists and built your production plant blocks away from the original design. You're putting people out of work Scrap; you following me?" he asked. I shook my head in agreement and realized why I was still alive. He was using a business proposition and no matter how fucked up it would sound I would have to agree to it if I wanted to walk outta there. "So what you saying Slick?" It's Ricky Slick mutha fucka! Don't you ever call me Slick. I'm a Boss nigga." He flashed like a cat wit gasoline in his ass. His whole demeanor changed; shit I thought I had fucked up completely. "Now this is what it's going to be; you can keep your blocks but you go re-up from me when that time comes. Face go have the work, it's go be at 17.5 you done fucked off these last months; you can work it down once you prove your loyalty to the machine. You follow me?" I was being squeezed like a sponge. Rock didn't even hit me over the head like that but at the end of it all I knew he wasn't gonna match what I was getting from Flaco anyway. I just needed to get out of there so I gave my word and Ricky Slick made sure I understood what that meant. "This is a contract, a verbal contract and if you renege just consider it the time of the season where anybody can get it… it will be a green light on your whole movement if you don't comply." I shook my head and Ricky Slick told Face "get this little mutha fucka outta here." The pillow case was then placed back over my head and my hands were zipped tied behind my back. They walked me back out to the garage and put me back in the Tahoe, moments later we pulled off.

Chocolate had now worked Vamp up to her level. He had chirped me over twenty times until he said fuck it. "If this Nigga$ don't chirp back in the next five minutes I'm waking shit up on Coconino." Everybody knew wasn't no stopping him once his mind was set so they all agreed. "Chocolate give me yo house keys." Vamp asked. She handed the house keys to Vamp and they were off as soon as the five minutes were up. The four of them hopped in Studder's Cutlass with the A.R.15 I kept in my room then disappeared into the neighborhood.

It was getting late and the ride back to my Cadi seemed longer than the ride to the stash house they had me in. I still questioned if I was really gonna make it out of this situation. When we came to a stop the pillow case came off along with the ties and from my laying down position I saw the trimming of the roof of the market where everything had started. "Make sure you do what you suppose to do or its nite nite nigga." The back opened up and I bounced out.

About the same time Hawk, Vamp, JBang and Studder were all in Studder's Cutlass pulling up on Coconino. "Aye my Nigga$ before you get to close let us bounce out so I can put this AR on these niggas." Vamp was ready to kill and Hawk and JBang were ready with him. "Just keep it at an easy coast Studder so we can get back in."

"Alright my Nigga$ I got you." Once the Coconino boys were in sight Vamp, Hawk and JBang used the Cutlass as a shield, opening up on everyone on the block. Flacka!Flacka!Flacka! Pop!Pop!Pop!Pop!Pop!Pop!Pop!Pop! Flacka!Flacka!Flacka!Flacka!Flacka!Flacka!Flacka!Flacka! Flacka! shots chased Lil Bone down and he crumbled like wax. "Bitch ass nigga Vamp shouted as he jumped back into the Cutlass behind Hawk. JBang sat up front with Studder who simply asked. "Where we going"? "Go to Chocolates my Nigga$" Vamp replied.

Once I hopped in my Cadi I was in possession of my Ruger. I thought to myself I should get on these niggas right now. I grabbed my churp and saw I missed 90 calls so I decided to get to the house first and let everyone know I was good. I pulled out of the market and noticed Bone on his cell phone in the passenger seat of the Tahoe. Dirty pulled the Tahoe out right behind me riding my bumper. I shook my head thinking what the fuck this nigga doing then I made a left on Pinal Vista from 36th street; he did the same then sped up on the side of me. Bones and Face windows came down then Pop! Pop!Pop!Pop!Pop!Pop!Pop!Pop! I swerved the Cadi off the road and into a fence then smack; it was darkness. When I came to my senses my Cadi was folded up on the side of a house; my mouth was bloody and I could barely see from the blood in my eye from my forehead being split. I could hear the Tahoe coming back around to finish me off. I climbed out the wreck making it down the alley where I tossed my Ruger in a garbage bin. I got two steps, maybe three into the street at the end of the alley then blacked out on Forgeus two blocks away from home. When I woke up I was in Kino Hospital lying in the bed tubes everywhere. Tubes in my nose, tubes in my arm and tubes in my dick. Chocolate sat in the recliner next to the bed; when she saw I was awake she started sobbing and kissing my cheek. My mom was on the other side of the bed looking at me with tears falling from her eyes. I already knew what she was thinking and there was nothing I could say to her to ease the pain and guilt she felt had caused this situation. Chocolate broke our silent communication saying "Oh daddy I thought you wasn't go make it. The police had the whole neighborhood shut down." I couldn't speak to her either but for an entirely different reason I was high as hell from the morphine. Her mouth was moving but I could barely hear what she was saying. I started trying to pull the tubes out of my nose and told her to "calm down calm down Chocolate! Help me get this shit off me." My mom found her voice and said "boy if you don't lie down and be still you will die. You were hit 3 times; once in your shoulder, once in your side and once in your back. You had to have surgery and they said one of your lungs was slightly damaged. Know that you will heal and you will be alright." I suddenly started feeling all the pain and knew she was right. I took a deep breath and that even hurt. "Where my Nigga$ at"? I asked.

"They all at my house; the hood was too hot for them to stay around. You know somebody got killed on Coconino." Chocolate had the look like she knew more than what she was saying but she wasn't go say no more. "What you talking about gimme the phone." She handed me the phone and said "I'm glad you alright daddy." As I put in the numbers to Vamp's chirp I was interrupted by a knock on the door and then an intrusion. "Sorry to disturb you I'm Detective Williams from the Tucson Police Department." He extended his hand towards my Mom, she shook it then he turned towards me with his hand and I just nodded my head. "Corey Carter or do you prefer I call you Scrap?"

"Man my name is Corey. I could already see where this was going. Williams was one of them special niggas, the kind who thought they were better than everybody especially his own kind. He probably hated he was black because everything about him screamed foothills or country club; but he had the spunk of someone who had been doing this awhile. "Ok Scrap, do you know who was shooting at you yesterday?"

"No, no I don't."

"Yeah somehow I already knew that was going to be your answer; so what do you know about Steve Jenkins or Lil Bone as you all call him."

"What about him I asked."

"He's dead Scrap and Bobby Wells is gonna be paralyzed from the waist down or should I say Wax?"

"Man I don't know nothing, I ain't heard nothing and I ain't seen nothing. I'm still wondering how I ended up in this hospital."

"Well you better figure it out fast, from the looks of things somebody didn't want you to wake up from this. "If you think of anything here's my card and I know all about the code of the streets; I already know you are not going to say anything but I gotta say it anyway." He held his hand out towards me and I looked at it like he was holding shit in his hands. I guess the look on my face pissed him off so Chocolate broke the tension. "I'll hold on to it sir. He is just upset because he just woke up. If he thinks of anything we will give you a call it's good to know you have Corey's best interest at heart." When Williams walked out my Mom said "well that was mighty white of you Chocolate." I was looking at Chocolate like she had lost her mind and she returned the look right back and started apologizing and tearing up the card with it ending up in the trash. "Daddy we at least gotta play it off; we don't need the police all in our mix." She was right but at the same time our motto was always fuck the police and they knew it.

I chirped Vamp. "What's good Choc?"

"This Scrap Nigga$."

"Awe shit whats good wit my Young Nigga$ you straight?"

"Yeah I'm good they got me doped up in this bitch. Them suckas hit me 3 times but I'm good what's up though?" Suddenly the door swung open, no knocks and it was Williams again. "Damn! Nigga$ you got hit 3 times?" Vamp's voice echoed in the room because of the loudspeaker. "Aye my Nigga$ I'm go chirp you back, I got company." "Alright my Nigga$." "Sorry about the intrusion again Scrap, I forgot to ask you about Mustapha Cook. You know Mumu and Daryl Turner or you might call him Cisco. I'm asking you because all this started happening when your house was shot up and all these bodies began dropping after that." "Man, I told you I don't know nothing now if you would excuse me; I'm trying to get some rest." He was walking out for the second time and happened to throw something into the trash can where he saw the ripped up card. He glanced back at Chocolate with a look that said I'm going to be watching both you mutha fuckas.

CHAPTER 16

When I was released from the hospital Chocolate was out front in her Honda. The nurse had wheeled me out to the main entrance and into the car. As we pulled off my thoughts went back to my stay in the hospital and how everything became clear to me. Vamp's decision to hit Coconino caused a chain reaction. Bone had got the call about his brother being dead as I was pulling out of the market. If Vamp would've made his decision anytime sooner I never would've made it out of the Tahoe or for that matter the stash house. It was as close to death as I wanted to be. We headed to my Moms' and I was paranoid as Chocolate navigated through the streets. I knew she felt my vibe because when we got to the border of the hood she reached in her purse and handed me her 25 caliber Ruger. I looked at it like what was this go do but kept hold of it until we pulled up to the house.

When I walked through the door my mother was in the living room praying with a member from her church. She had dived all the way in by now. I teased her when we would be alone calling her a holy roller. On cue she said "Scrap sit down with us and pray." "Mama I ain't got time for that right now." "Prayer just might help you change your mind and your direction; He did it for me, He'll do it for you; a little prayer certainly won't hurt baby." I shook my head and walked into my room; I needed to smoke some weed bad. She followed me right in. "Scrap I want you to know how I feel about all that shooting and foolishness y'all do- ing in these streets and bringing it up on my doorstep." "I know Mama." I cut her off because I had heard it all before. "Well if you know, then you have got to do something about it. Seeing you laid up in the hospital like that really scared me; these niggas are crazy Corey! I was thinking it may be safer for all of us if you weren't in sight, you know right here in the middle of the mix; so why don't you move in with Chocolate?" I couldn't believe it; she was kicking me out and trying to be polite about it. "If that's what you want Mama I'll go and be out yo way." "No Corey you are never in my way I just don't want to see you hurt anymore." I knew that everything she said was true and I also knew it would be best because anything could happen in the blink of an eye and I didn't want to put my Mom at risk especially when she had herself together, for the most part.

I packed most of my belongings and was off to the East side moving in with Chocolate. She wanted this bad and I had a feeling she had played a part in this happening. All she did was smile; she knew she had me full time now. I called my Nigga$ and had them pull up on me at Chocolate's then explained the whole get down. The hood was still on fire, the police were everywhere so the blocks were shut down though we knew that would only be for so long. "It's really on with these niggas" Hawk stated."

"Hell yeah and I got something for all they asses" Vamp replied.

When I was laid up in the hospital, thoughts of murder filled my mind; it consumed me until I came up with a plan and I only needed one person to understand where I was coming from. If he went for it the hood would be ours. "Yeah my Nigga$ its on wit these niggas so be on your shit; don't get caught slippin. I'm sure the green light has been given for all of us." I'll be out here now and I gotta get a new whip so until then I'll be push'n Chocolate's shit. Hit my chirp when the police leave and then we can get back to it. When that time comes I'll meet you on 22nd at the Bottle Shop. After I get my whip you know I'm back on the block." With that they was gone and I hopped my wounded ass into traffic to piece more of the puzzle together.

CHAPTER 17

I chirped Flaco. "Que onda Scrap?"

"Aye shit you already know, you in town?"

"Yeah I'm at Mariscos right now eating."

"Oh alright can I pull up on you? It's important."

"Yeah I'm at the one in Central on 22nd."

"Alright give me about 10 minutes."

"I'll be here."

When I pulled up to the Mexican Seafood restaurant it wasn't that crowded. I parked next to Flaco's truck then struggled to get out of the compact Honda. The seats that were filled had eyes all on me; as I struggled I realized I was still wrapped up in the bandage looking and moving like I had been through hell. I found Flaco sitting in a corner booth with someone he introduced as his Primo. "What's up Scrap? you should be resting, man."

"I'm good Flaco, I'll be alright."

"You hungry? I'm gonna order you something; you'll love it. Primo get him the Ceviche and corn tortillas." Primo hopped up and stood behind the two customers in front of him. "So Scrap what up what's so important?"

"As you can see I got a situation."

"Yes I see that."

"But its nothing that can't be solved. I was thinking with you being a businessman an all you might consider my proposal." Primo ordered the food then started to walk towards us but Flaco held his hand up to stop him and said "order him the Horchata with it." I was thinking he didn't want Primo to hear the details of the business. "So let's hear it Scrap."

"Simply put, I need some Mafioso style shooters. I need someone to send a wrecking ball down Coconino and take everything out. I know we do good business and I know we will continue to do good business with Coconino out of the way. We can jump our profit another 2 kilos. I know that's small time to you but I'm trying to get there you feel me."

"You know what Scrap I like you. You see yourself as just what you are a businessman and I was doing the same as you when I was your age. You gotta make moves to get ahead; how do you think I got to where I am taking orders? Hell nah I took my position, just remember nothing comes easy and sacrifices have to be made and nothing is free; it all comes with a price." I shook my head then asked. "So what are you saying Flaco?"

"I'm saying it's gonna cost you 30 grand and when these guys pull up on Coconino it won't be a problem anymore." 30 grand wasn't an issue as much as parting with it was. But Rock's words echoed in my head as Flaco and I shook hands. "You playing with the big boys now." Primo came back to the table with my meal. I squeezed the lime over my tortillas and went to work on it like I had been locked in someone's prison. After we parted ways I headed to my safe to get Flaco's money and get my Mom out of the hood for a minute. "A trip to Cali right now Scrap!"

"Yeah Mama I already have your ticket with some spending money for you and Grams, Goldie and Lucky, y'all have a good time and I'll take care of everything here for you."

"You know that's sweet and all but I smell a dead cat on the line; what are you not telling me?"

"Nothing Mama except Chocolate will pick you up tomorrow and take you to the airport okay so be ready. I love you Mama, see you when you get back."

"Love you too Corey and thank you baby and stay safe, don't let the streets catch your ass out." In my head I was already there. Coconino would never be the same cause when it's on it's on.

I ended up purchasing a SC 400 Lexus after Flaco was taken care of. I was done with the old schools. I needed something that would get up as soon as I hit the gas. I ended up trading Chocolate's Civic and paying the rest in cash. It was used but only had 20,000 miles so I was happy; Chocolate was too because I told her it was hers. After the paperwork was done for the Lexus I went straight to the hood. I passed down all the blocks seated low behind the Lexus tints. When I came to the Coconino and Cochise intersection I said "Fuck it!" and turned down Coconino, as I passed the spot where everyone was I could see the necks breaking trying to see who I was. I came up to Forgeus, made a left and was out of sight. Chocolate looked at me and said "you just had to do that huh." I grinned at her and just gave her my famous dirty old man laugh.

The hood was open for business; the police was gone for the time being so I hit the Young Nigga$ on the chirp and told them to open the blocks back up. "Watch them niggas on Coconino they out there real thick." Y'all got a good week to get it then its go be hot again."

"What you talking about Scrap?"

"I'm talking bout it's about to go down so get your bread up, you got a week." My Nigga$ wanted all the info in detail so I set up a meeting on Hawks block. When I pulled up all the Young Nigga$ was on the corner grinding. Hawk, JBang, Vamp and Studder were in the house. "Whats good wit my Nigga$?"

"Awe shit young Scrap is back."

"That you flex'n in the Lex? My Nigga$ that bitch is clean."

"Yeah that's Chocolate's shit."

"Oh it's Chocolates! Let me find out she put it on you like that JBang said." I laughed and we all sat down in the living room. "I set it up on the DL to get real funky around here next week. I want y'all and the rest of the Young Nigga$ to grind hard this week then we go shut it down. Them boys are going to be all over this bitch this time and I promise you they ain't gonna give nobody no breathing room. I put a price on the Coconino niggas." Vamp was the first to ask. "You put a price on em Nigga$, how much?"

"Don't worry about it, just know next week they go get the business Mafioso style."

"Shit Scrap they could've killed you my Nigga$ we'd of done the shit for free and you know we will."

"Don't trip my Nigga$ it's still go be some fish to fry but we go send a wrecking ball through there first to knock all that shit down." We all smiled at the possibility of shutting down Coconino for good; causing pain to my enemies was a thought that felt as good as the money that was coming in. This was the point of no return, actually way past it. Everyone was with the plan; as long as Coconino didn't strike first we was good. All of us were pulling all-nighters the whole week then we shut it down. We planned on taking our girls to the movies and dinner when the "construction workers" showed up making sure we kept all receipts tracking our whereabouts. I knew Williams was going to be sniffing around trying to capture loose crumbs when this hell brakes.

Around 8:42 pm I got the text from Flaco. It read X marks the spot. I never responded I just popped popcorn into my mouth and sipped my Icee with Chocolate right under my arm watching a scary flick. On Coconino it was more than a scary flick. Face, Bone, Trigg, BooBear, Ty and a few more Coconino boys posted in front of the trap house waiting for the next sale looked up and a caravan of Dodge pickups pulled up the block blasting their Mexican music to the max. All the trucks pulled up slowly and had dark tint to where you could barely see the outline of the driver. When all three trucks stopped in line with the trap house Face stood up and said. "What the fuck is they doing?" The music screamed through the woofers then suddenly came to a dead silence in all three trucks. "Man see what the fuck they on Ty." As Ty stood up and took a few steps towards the trucks two shooters rose from the bed of each truck holding A.R. 15's with the drum. "Awe shit!" Face shouted as he made his exit around the side of the house. Bone was right on his heels trying to escape the swarm of bullets that riddled the porch and house. Flacka! Flacka! Flacka! Flacka! Flacka! Flacka! Flacka! Flacka! Flacka! Flacka! Flacka! Flacka! Shots spun Ty around leaving him in an awkward position twisted on the ground. Flacka! Flacka! Flacka! Flacka! Flacka! Flacka! Trigg folded two steps off the porch trying to follow Face and Bone. Flacka! Flacka! Flacka! Flacka! Flames caught BooBear as he tried to return fire but it jammed up after two shots leaving him on his back and elbows looking at the stars. Over 200 rounds were fired, 3 were dead and 2 injured. ET and Slim both caught grazes that looked like direct hits. The unknown Mexicans pulled off blasting their music leaving the same way they pulled up and disappeared into the darkness of the neighborhood. When Face and Bone came from the back of the house all they saw were bodies and blood. Face lowered his head and simply said. "Call the ambulance my nigga."

CHAPTER 18

Detective Williams slammed the files of Cisco, Loon, Danger, Mumu and Lil Bones on top of his desk after being chewed out by his superior and mugging his partner as he was told there would be 3 more bodies added to his caseload. "These sons of bitches are going to pay." This is what he told himself as he attempted to fit the pieces of the puzzle together. Walking out of his office he rounded up all the officers in the gang units and said "I want Corey Carter aka Scrap, Vincent Brown aka Vamp, Hakeem Harris aka Hawk, Jason Smith aka JBang and Stacey Woods aka Studder all brought in for questioning. One of the rookie patrolmen asked "under what grounds?" Williams almost popped his top and replied "under the grounds of 8 dead motherfuckers.. just get their asses in here. Get the hell out of my face and do your F'n job. In fact I'll tell you what I want." He got everyone's attention with that statement; the patrolmen, the sergeants and the gang unit. He went to the map on the wall that highlighted criminal activity and gang involvement and placed a special pin in the area Western Hills is located. "As of now

Western Hills is on zero tolerance. I want a command center right in the heart of it and I want car, foot and bike patrol on 24 hr shifts every day. I want answers if someone shits; I want to know about it. They won't know what hot is until they really feel the heat and we're about to bring it!"

Williams slammed the door so hard to his office the glass rattled prompting swift movement from the other officers to get to work and start making things happen. The blocks were officially hotter than fish grease. If you came outside you got harassed. Some of the young Nigga$ would go to Juvi only to get out and go right back. If you were caught wearing any type of red you were stopped, checked for warrants and searched before you were free to go. After about a month of harassment the Western Hill residents had had enough of the tactics the Tucson police officers were using. They had forced Mrs. Turner, the grandmother of a known Western Hills member to lay face down on the floor of her living room on a trumped up raid claiming they had mistakenly raided the wrong house. This forced everyone's hand in the neighborhood. Hispanic and Black families had had enough. They marched hand in hand to the Downtown headquarters and protested until the news trucks showed up. Once that happened somebody had to come out and answer questions. By the 5th week the Zero tolerance was lifted and the command center was gone.

"Aye my Nigga$ I just slid through the hood let's get this money the boys is gone." Studder was ready to get back to it but I was still skeptical; we had been on the low for so long I knew the police was looking for us. "I don't know my Nigga$ I think we should give it a little more time."

"Fuck that Scrap you know scared money don't make none."

"You damn right, fuck it lets get back to it then; call the homies tell them its good. I'll get with y'all in the hood." Studder got his Young Nigga$ working and JBang, Vamp and Hawk did the same. Something spiritually was still pulling at me though; to do what my first mind said. By the time I pulled up to the hood I lost that feeling and I was back to thinking it was a good day to get some money. As I turned left off of Kaibab to pull into my Mom's driveway I saw 3 unmarked squad cars right behind me. I hopped out the Lexus and two officers were right on me. "Corey Carter, we have to detain you, you're code 11."

"Code 11! What the fuck is a code 11?" One officer was placing me in cuffs when the younger one said "wanted for questioning." The door opened and my mom stood in the doorway, bible in hand shaking her head and not missing a beat railing at the officers "that no one is without sin so don't be so bent on pointing a finger when you've got three pointing back at you."

"Mama go back inside the house before they try to cuff you too."

"They might try" was all she said after looking them up and down; then she turned and walked into the house with the door slamming behind her. The officers drove me in silence to the Santa Cruz substation located on South Park. I thought the other two unmarked cars would follow but they were gone as soon as we pulled off my block. Once they got me inside I was placed in an interrogation room. It had a surveillance camera in the upper corner that brought back a memory of Ricky Slick's stash house. I figured T.P.D.

had a detective recording and watching the monitor for any movement patterns, expressions or any telltale signs. Thinking they had me right where they wanted me; mind you I was cuffed tight to a table in a hot ass room with no A/C. The only thing they were able to observe was me going to sleep. This must've pissed off Williams because he busted through the door in a rage "wake the fuck up Corey this ain't the Hampton Inn." I looked up to see him signal to whoever was on the monitor to cut the camera; then he attacked all my pressure points while I was still cuffed to the table practically growling in my ear saying "Yeah Scrap how you like that? Real up close and personal like them bodies you left on Coconino."

"Fuck you Williams" I shouted through the pain.

"Shut the fuck up Scrap you're going down. I got all your boys lined up and they couldn't wait to hand your ass over. The fat one sang before he reached the station, so let's hear it; where were you the night all hell broke loose?"

"I was sitting at a table with the devil and your wife, you punk mutha fucka. You need to shut the hell up and get outta my face. I really put some extra on it and spat on the wall and said "fuck you Williams". Oh he hated that because as my Mama would say "he retched back and slapped the shit outta me." I was trying to shake him, even in my limitations I was able to head butt him and his hands started closing around my throat. He choked me until I saw stars and felt darkness calling my name. I vaguely heard a door open and he was hauled off me by two plain clothes officers.

"That's enough Williams, that's enough dammit."

"I'm suing you mutha fucka's."

"Shut the fuck up boy!" One of the officers shouted as they pushed Williams out of the room. I took my licks and about 10 hours later the door opened and two uniformed officers came and uncuffed me.

"Mr. Carter you're free to go."

"Oh I can go now after y'all done assaulted me, kept me in here all day on some fake ass bullshit." Walking out to the property desk Vamp, Studder, Hawk and JBang were standing in line waiting for their property looking like Williams had got to them too. We were all released to Vamps grandmother because my mom was still on parole and we were minors.

"What's good you straight Scrap?" Vamp asked.

"Yeah I'm good my Nigga$. Williams just got to me while I was cuffed to the table."

"Man fuck Williams I wanna do something."

"Boy watch your mouth curse'n like you grown." Vamps grandma wasn't that old and she knew what we was into; all she could say was "y'all be careful out there, I hope and pray you realize soon God's plan for you and see this is not it; all you need to hear is one word from Him for a revolution to light up inside each and every one of you. All this will do is bring death to your door or a jail sentence and please believe one or the other is just fine with them. Then she said, "now get your little asses outta my car before I get shot at."

CHAPTER 19

We had made it through the storm and the hood was officially ours. Coconino was on operation shut down and the Young Niagg$ was out and had every block pumping like tomorrow wasn't coming. All you saw in the hood was Yankee ball caps, even young people who wasn't on the block yet had on some type of NY gear. The movement was in full effect and everybody knew if a Coconino boy popped up give him the business. That was the law on every block ran by the Young Nigga$.

I patrolled the hood dropping packages and stacking my bread. I learned from my mama if you be ready you don't have to get ready. So I was always on swivel and watching for the drop I knew was coming. It was just a matter of time with Ricky Slick plotting to get back what he felt was his. But the more we hustled the stronger we became with more young niggas leaving the Boys and Girls club to hustle on the block. We had the numbers and the money just kept coming. This was when I truly realized what Rock had told me about the money and power. The law was shoot on site on anyone who threatened to take what we had built. So if you hustled you had to have a weapon. We wasn't waiting for Coconino to strike back, we were looking for them to pop up. The whole outfit of Western Hills was changed and Ricky Slick had no choice but to respect it. Them young boys was out there on some real shit and it was maxed out intense with them clutching their pistols ready to fire on anything and anyone that moved wrong. With Face shadowing Slick he says "Kill him when he slips up."

On an evening I would be usually busy it turned out to be slow. All my Nigga$ posted in the hood trying to find the next sale and I was bored so I called Chocolate. "What's up baby?"

"Nothing daddy, what's going on?"

"I'm just seeing what's good wit you."

"Oh you must be bored huh?"

"Why you say it like that? Like I can't call to see how you doing."

"Nigga when was the last time you did that?"

"What's up is Bobby working the door?"

"I think so, why?"

"I'm go come up there and see you while I can; it's slow right now."

"Alright, you coming right now?"

"Imma try to, I'll call when I'm outside." I hopped in the Lexus coupe and pushed up 22nd until I came to the Candystore. When I pulled into the lot and parked I rolled myself a blunt and smoked before I called Chocolate. From where I sat facing the double doors to the club I could watch everybody coming and going. It was a weekday so it wasn't really packed. As I smoked and listened to the music inside the club the doors swung open and a thick light toned redbone walked out holding two bags and her purse. She wore heels that gave her an extra 3 to 5 inches and she was glowing even though the sun had already set. Her booty shorts showed her thick figure allowing her toned legs to be showcased like a downhill skier and right then I knew for certain this was some good weed cause I was ready to go buy some snow in hot ass Arizona. Her blouse was buttoned at the bottom but the top was close to bursting aggressively from those 36D cups. I watched her spot the Lexus like she smelled the Kush I was burning. She walked over to my window and tapped it. I cracked it just enough to let smoke slap her in the face. "What's up Scrap?" she asked. You know that was fucked up how you did me; I had a present for you and everything." She stood on the side of the Lexus with her ass and lips poked out like only a stripper knows how to do. I really looked at her and realized this was Diamond. Damn she was bad the night of my birthday but outside in the open; she was on a whole nutha level. She was a gift alone and she knew it. "What's good Diamond?" What you talking about you never called?"

"Yeah I had some problems with that shit; I'm here now what you got up tonight?"

"Hold on." She ran in front of the Lexus and kept going a few cars down then put her bags in her car. She then came back to the passenger side of the Lexus and got in. "OK let's go." She was ready and looking like a million. I pulled off from the Candystore thinking to myself if Chocolate only knew. I drove down 22nd until I came to the drive thru liquor store. "Let me get a pint of that Remy VS, a pack of back-woods and two Red Bulls." When the Chino came back to the window with my items I paid then pulled off. Diamond had reclined her seat back and we were in traffic. "Yo Lex is nice Scrap, I like this. I had heard about what happened to your Cadi and how you crashed it. I wanted to go see you in the hospital but that would've been crazy right?"

"You know you wasn't finna come see me girl." As I came up to 22nd and Alvernon I noticed the De Anza drive-in was open so I pulled into the small line to see what was showing. After we agreed on what flick to check out we eased over the humps and found a space to park. I twisted a couple of blunts and reclined my seat.

Diamond was cool, we talked about all kinds of meaningless shit as we sat smoking and drinking and watching the screen from time to time. She was sexy under the night glow but I kept it real boss. She was choosing on me and then my chirp went off. It was Chocolate. "Whats up daddy are you comin up here?" "Naw Ma, I got caught up and I got to make a few runs. I'll be up there to get you though." She was upset but didn't let it get to her. She knew I was about my money. "Alright daddy I'll see you when you get here."

"Alright then I'll be up there at 2. When I hung up Diamond was like "look at Chocolate trying to play her position; I can play it better though. If I'm on the pole doing my thang for us then I don't need you in the club because if you there I'm most likely to be relaxing and this ain't no spa and bath, no country club shit. If you coming to get me I'll do all the relaxing I need then, I'm just saying though."

"What you saying?" I asked.

"Bitches don't know what they got till it's gone and it's gone because they let the side piece take the number one spot. When it's worth it I'll play the #2 just because I know it ain't a bitch on this planet that'll make you feel like I will. I know that I will eventually be the #1 cuz I'm the real deal all-star." She passed me the backwood then went for my zipper and took me to a place me and my Young Nigga$ call Jawmacca. By the time the flick was over we was wasted. If the coupe was bigger we would have been doing some thangs but she had too much body in too little a space so we rain checked on that. When I pulled back into the Candystore it was established that Diamond was my side bitch. She reached into her purse and cashed me out telling me "don't worry about nothing Scrap I got you; I'll get you a key made to my crib and everything. You come when-ever you feel like it alright baby?" With that she hopped her sexy ass out the Lexus but not before she kissed me on the cheek. Diamond was only 18 but had a body that would make a 30 year old jealous. Even though Chocolate was only 20 she was a lot more mature; you could tell she had learned a lot from the people she had dealt with prior to me. As for Diamond she was more of a livewire who knew the game and chose to play it. We clicked instantly but Chocolate was my main, she had been down with me since day one.

When Diamond pulled off she beep beep her horn twice then slipped off into traffic. I sat in the Lexus faded shaking my head thinking I was the coldest Nigga$ on the planet, moments later Chocolate chirped. "You outside daddy?"

"Yeah I'm out here."

"Alright I just gotta pay the DJ then I'm coming alright!" I hung up then hopped into the passenger seat and leaned back. It was like as soon as Diamond got out I started spinning; when Chocolate got in I could tell something was wrong because she was all smiles until she sat behind the wheel.

"Who you had up in here Scrap got it smelling all fruity and shit?"

"What! Man pull off you tripp'n."

"Oh I'm trip'n and I guess my eyes are bad too cause I'm pretty damn sure that's lip gloss all on yo cheek but I'm trip'n right? Who you been letting kiss on you Scrap?"

"Trying to play it off I asked her," "What the hell you talk'n bout?"

"Oh you don't know what I'm talk'n bout?. O.K. nigga ok." With that she cranked up the engine put the car in drive and sped out of the parking lot and into the night weaving in and around any car she came close to. That was the longest ride ever. She was steaming and quiet, a dangerous combo for any brother. I knew I had slipped up again but I was so wasted I didn't give a damn so we rode in silence.

The next few nights I found myself spending more time with Diamond because Chocolate was on one every night about who I let kiss me. One particular night Hawk was at the house when she in full battle gear. I decided to flip the script so I gave Hawk the look of lets bounce and headed to the hood where I hoped there was less drama. We crept through the backstreets of the Eastside. Hawk was reclined in the passenger seat as I turned corner after corner through an residential area; suddenly Hawk rose up in the seat saying "aye my Nigga$ you see that?"

"Naw what was it?"

"Double back around I think I spotted something." It was late Wednesday night; already after midnight which my Mama called the devil's hours. When I circled back around the block coming down the same street, we both spotted it this time "bingo" Hawk stated as I slowly eased pass Bone's Cadillac. He was parked with the motor running under a carport. His brake lights were on and smoke was coming from the exhaust. I parked about four houses from where he was parked and grabbed my pistol; Hawk did the same and followed behind me. We crept up close enough to notice it was Bone sitting in the driver seat like he was waiting for something or someone then Pop!pop!pop!pop!pop!pop! pop!pop!pop! Fireworks light up the carport like the fourth of July. We unloaded fast and disappeared but not before hearing screams of a woman as we hopped into the Lexus. I headed back east to Chocolates not because I wanted to but because it was a lot closer. Hawk passed out on the couch and I put Chocolate to sleep with some make up sex. The next morning we dropped Hawk off on his block then pulled up to my Mom's to check on her. When we walked through the door she was watching the news update. "Last night on the East side of town, Ronald "Bone" Wilkins was gunned down in his girlfriend's carport as he waited for her. If you have any information please call 88-Crime, police have no leads but say it appears to be gang related. "Did they say Ronald Wilkins?" Chocolate asked my Mom.

"Yes I believe they did say that name."

"I went to school with him; isn't he from over here daddy?" I shook my head like I couldn't believe what I had just heard. "Yeah that's fucked up, that's the homie." That was all my Mom needed to hear she changed the channel to her stories but not before talking a little shit. "These Negroes are killing each other like they getting paid for each head that rolls; it's a damn shame, all the police have to do is sit back and wait for us to kill each other off then they won't have to do it. This is Arizona black people, the last state I know of to acknowledge Martin Luther King's birthday as a national holiday and yet to acknowledge him as a man. It's no secret how they feel about us and they don't try to hide it. Ask any minority what their state motto is for us? It's come on vacation and leave on probation. Arizona's Penitentiaries are filled to the brim with repetitive Blacks and Latinos and it's by design make no mistake; and they flourish by setting the system up to ensure that you will be back. We have to learn to care what matters to each other; and more importantly that we learn how to care about ourselves. Plant the seed so we can root and grow strong vines. Think about this. How can we stand up for ourselves, for each other if there's nobody left standing?"

"Sadly my Mom was right and there I stood in it, shit deep in it." I let Chocolate take the Lexus to work and chilled with my Mom until she got tired of me; that's what I would tell her when I was ready to go but I wouldn't say goodbye to her. I don't know why I just never said it to her even when we were on the phone bout to hang up. I just said "love you Mama" and she'd say "love you too Scrap, be careful." I had Vamp come pick me up and take me to Hawks block. As soon as I pulled up Hawk was cheesin. "We got that nigga Scrap."

"Oh you heard?"

"Hell yeah the hood buzz'n right now."

Then Vamp interrupted "oh that was y'all man why you didn't tell me y'all was on a mission?"

"Shit my Nigga$ we just stumbled on it."

"Yeah I was wondering why y'all didn't pull up last night."

"Well now you know I said sarcastically." Ricky Slick kept taking losses. We thought that because it had happened on the East side it would take some of the heat off of us; it didn't because we were still the center of his attention. Bone's death was so unexpected that he demanded answers but all that came out his mouth was "I know it was that young muthafucka."

CHAPTER 20

Flaco and Scrap's friendship had grown and it felt similar to a mob like relationship based around business. Flaco took interest in me because he loved how I did my thang. Watching me grow reminded him of how he started coming up from Mexico with basically nothing and now being a major factor in the Sinaloa Cartel and a legitimate business-man at the same time. Flaco knew I would have to get my hand in the legit pot if I wanted to clean up my money; so he made me an offer. "Que onda Scrap?"

"Awe it ain't shit what's good Flaco?" I replied as I hopped into his Chevy Silverado that sat on 28 inch Lexani's. We pulled off and I was thinking Flaco was just tired of his crew so he wanted to hit a corner or two with the young fly Nigga$. Today Flaco was all business; he wore a midnight black Armani suit with black custom gator boots, oh he was clean. "What you all dressed up for Flaco? You look like you on your way to your sister's Quincenera or something."

He laughed at my joke then got serious.

"No my friend, today I'm going to show you a property on the Northwest side in the Warehouse District."

"Property! What for?"

He smiled then said "Just wait." When we pulled into the Warehouse District we parked and walked into a building that had construction going on all around it. Once inside I spotted the outfit of a night club coming to life. The bar stretched across the room. Balconies and poles were being constructed and the stage and lights were being set up like a Broadway production. "What you think about this Scrap?"

"Man this is going to be nice Flaco, real nice." We walked through more doors that led down a narrow hallway and then to an office area. Flaco found a seat behind a nice desk that sat centered in the room. He fumbled through a box on the desk that held Cuban cigars. He was feeling himself completely as he clipped the tip of his cigar, leaned back and placed his Gators on the desk. "Scrap my friend, you're a boss right?" I nodded in agreement about to make a comment and he cut me off and said "not to take anything away from what you were about to say but I'm a fucking boss Scrap! You see this shit Scrap? This is my first establishment from the ground up. I've partnered with many people, people in a totally different world than what you and I have been involved in getting our capital together to make this kind of move. From local restaurateurs, boxing and concert promoters to privately owned meat markets that have had success because they went organic are now my partners. I knew the time was right to incorporate these businesses for the sole purpose of cleaning my money; I did that and now what you are looking at is 100% all mine. This club is my dream and here we sit in the office behind the scene of what's going to be the hottest spot in town.

I can't lie I was amazed at the energy that came from Flaco as he told his story. It was like my eyes were extended to a wider screen, a bigger picture so to speak. It was the same feeling I had when I sold my first pack of dope and looked at the money pile on my bed. Hearing Flaco explain his vision let me know it was levels to everything and I was still at the bottom no matter how I tried to look at it.

"Scrap I like you, you're not afraid to take a risk and you're loyal. I know you're only going to last in the street game for so long before you get killed or are in jail. While you're ahead right now I want to give you an opportunity to clean your money like it was given to me. What do you think of being my partner?"

"Partner! What do you mean, with this?"

"Yeah I'm talking about this club right here right now."
"How much I have to put up and how much of a partner will I be?"

"You see that's why I like you Scrap; you're young but you're smart. Most people would say yeah and not even know the numbers, but not you, you're a natural born hustler and might not even know it. I'm thinking 25% for 250."

"Two fifty!"

"C'mon Scrap, look at the places we have club hopped from time to time. They're the so-called hot spots of the town, no ours is going to be a huge upgrade. This is the Warehouse District with a venue that will hold at least 500 plushed out to the max with something special and different on both floors capacity parking included. The V.I.P.'s bonus area will include access to specialties and will be served right here by the baddest girls you'll ever want to lay eyes on.

There will be no place like it and when the time is right we can start looking for prime property on the West Coast. "Really Big Thangs is bout to get started up in here Flaco but two fifty? Everything is negotiable right?" Flaco pulled his feet off the desk, ashed his cigar then sat up so I could understand exactly what he meant. "25% two hundred! Don't bullshit me Scrap I know you got it; now or never." All I could do was smile. "Can I at least name the joint Flaco?"

"Name it, what would you call it Scrap?" as he leaned back in his chair and smiled at my request.

"I'd call it The Kush Lounge, that's what I would call it."

"Damn Scrap! I like the sound of that." When we walked out of the club we were in agreement for 200 for 25%. Three months later it was opening night. All the promotions had the Kush Lounge the hottest spot in town. I couldn't wait to start getting my money back because that two hundred had me down like Rodney King. I still had to supply the blocks and I was using what they came up with to re-up. Because I was still a minor my name wasn't legally on any of the paperwork but I did collect the 25% every month and I learned how this side of the game goes. I had my own personal VIP booth and all access to everything, plus my own key to the office and one of the two safes inside. At this time you couldn't tell me shit after my first two years I had earned back what I invested; now the money was all profit and the whole town had the Scrap buzz. Flaco enjoyed his success and we toasted to what we felt was the good life. I was settled in my routine, Ricky Slick was a mystery and my Young Nigga$ was all eating. I was going to be turning

18 and had a whole lot going for me but it was something always missing so I decided to take a trip to California so my family could see the man I had become.

Chocolate didn't know it but it was a last minute decision to either take her or Diamond. Chocolate only made the cut because I didn't want to hear it when I got back. She was already complaining about how she wanted to work at the Kush Lounge but I had Diamond over there so Chocolate was left at the Candystore. It was coming to be a constant problem so she needed this trip to calm down. After the bags were packed we made our way to the airport. Every block in the hood was left with a brick and a half. I needed no excuses of running out of dope. When I dropped Vamp off his pack, he asked "damn Scrap how long you going to be gone." I didn't plan on staying for no longer than a week but who knew; I had enough money to do whatever I wanted. This was a surprise trip to Cali so when the airplane touched down in Oakland nobody was there to pick us up. I had reserved a rental car in Chocolates name so by the time I grabbed the luggage Chocolate had the rental keys to a new Cadi. We loaded it up with our bags then punched the address into the navigation system and hopped into the traffic. Once we reached Richmond city limits I knew exactly where I was. Every block I turned I explained to Chocolate what use to go down there. I showed her all my hangouts but once I got in the flats the feeling of homecoming hit me like a ton of bricks. I was right down the hill from my grandmother's house. In fact I could see her house from where I had parked in front of my cousins at the bottom of the hill. There were two individuals standing in the front yard smoking. They both were looking at the Cadi like who the hell is that. I hopped out and walked towards them. Every step I took they became more familiar; looking like an older version of my cousins Twanny and Joe. As I walked up on them I guess I got to close for comfort for Joe who drawed his weapon and asked "nigga who is you?"

All I could say was "nigga its me your cousin; you front'n like you don't know me."

"Scrap that you? Twanny hollered ``Aww shit Joe that's Scrap."

"Boy!" Joe said while shaking his head then we all embraced and I reunited with my aunts and younger relatives who were now running the block after their older brothers went to San Quintin. "Have you been up the hill to see your Grannie yet?" my aunt asked.

"I'm about to head up there next. I just had to stop right here; you know that Aunty." I introduced Chocolate and we all kicked it smoking and drinking. When I said my good-byes they knew I'd be back because this was my family and where I learned the little I did know about the streets before I moved to Arizona.

When we pulled into my Grandmother's driveway I re-membered all the events that had happened in the driveway alone. As I sat in the car with Chocolate here I was again reliving the memories and she was just as excited hearing them as I was telling them. She sat with them big brown eyes glued to every word I said. I was ready to see my Grandmother now and said "C'mon let's go." Walking up to the door I pushed the doorbell and heard a sound that made me smile. I could hear the locks unlatching and a voice saying "who is it?"

"Open the door" I shouted rudely in a way the person

on the other side would know it was me; when the door swung open my sister Goldie stood behind the wrought iron saying "boy I knew it was you as soon as I heard that. You're the only one who says that, like you have no home training at all." She opened the wrought iron and gave me a big hug while eyeing Chocolate so I introduced them in a hurry because my sister is messy when it came to the girls in my life. "Where's Grannie at Goldie?" I asked.

"You know she's in her room watching either Jeopardy or Wheel of Fortune or exercising with Jack LaLane. I'm going to go and surprise her; show Chocolate my room so she can put our stuff up."

"Yo room!" Well Lucki got your old room now so you're going to have to take his."

"Well he Lucki alright because if this wasn't just a vacation he'd have to let go of it."

"Boy you crazy! C'mon girl let me show you y'all room."

"I'm just play'n and don't you tell Lucki I said that either, he'll think I was serious."

"No he won't, he acts just like you when it comes to the pranks and jokes. He drives Grams crazy but she loves it and laughs at it all. I think she enjoys it because it reminds her of you Corey." I could hear the TV playing from the other side of her door. I walked in and she was laid up on the bed dozing in and out. I stood at the end of her bed until she felt the presence of someone. "Hey Gramma!" She fixed her eyes to the light and the glare coming off the TV and asked "Lucki why haven't you been in here to watch Jeopardy with me?"

I walked over to the side of her bed so she could see me better and said "you know Arizona is a little far to be traveling for Jeopardy night." As soon as she realized who I was she busted up laughing. "Corey! Oh Corey look at you, come here and let me hold you baby. I missed you; Lord have mercy I prayed you were safe down there in hellzona; you know that's what I call Arizona; it's just too hot down there. Now here you are all grown up and look at you you're so handsome; when did you get here Corey?" Don't bother telling me a lie and that you just got here because I know you already stopped by to see your hooligan cousins." I busted up laughing then and said "dang gramma I forgot how sharp you are because that's exactly what I was going to say. You look good gramma, is everything ok with you?"

"Yes, yes I've been fine baby now help me up I'm going to make you something to eat."

"Nah nah nah Gramma you relax and let me know later where you want to go and eat something or if you want to stay in I'll go and get it for you, just let me know okay." "Well alright then, look at you all take charge I like that Corey." I sat with my grandma until she fell asleep. She had me pulling out picture albums and everything else she could think of. She didn't want me to leave so Goldie went and picked up the food and we ate, laughed and even shed a few tears over the family members that had gone on. By the time she had dozed off it was after midnight when I tucked her in and kissed her forehead. My little brother still wasn't home so I asked Goldie "where Lucki at Goldie?"

"Hell you of all people should know where he's at. That nigga come in when he feel like it. Ringing any bells, Scrap? Hustlin I think it's called just like what I heard you been doing." Chocolate glanced at me and Goldie caught her and said. "Don't try and act like you don't, you know Mama go

tell it like the Lord said it." We all busted up laughing and
fired up the backwood on the porch. Around 1:30 I spotted
my little brother walking up the hill; after we embraced and
gave each other the shit I introduced him to Chocolate. As
we were talking and catching up I realized this wasn't the
little brother who was in camp when I left going to Arizona.
He was now another young life that was being groomed by
the rough and grimy streets of the Bay Area. Yeah Richmond
was the Base where it all started but it definitely was different and so was my brother. I explained to him how well I
was doing in AZ and all he saw is what he wanted for himself. I respected that because he was his own man; but I let
him know I had his back on whatever he needed. That's all
he needed was a plug with some primo work and I had the
best quality of it right from the border. He made a few orders
and he was ready to blow it up. The Cali experience was
going good, we took Gramma to her favorite restaurant, my
little brother was good and my sister was good. By this time
Chocolate was acting like she wanted to stay. It had been
two weeks Chocolate and I were standing on Pier 39 in San
Francisco when I got a call from Studder. "Aye my Nigga$ I
know you on vacation but you need to get back ASAP."

"Why what's good?" "Aye my Nigga$ I ain't finna get into
all of it on this line but I'm saying you should get back. "Alright
my Nigga$ I'll be back in two days." I hung up and left the
piers and headed back to Richmond to pack my bags. Once
my flight was booked I sat back and contemplated what it
could be. Ricky Slick, the police, it could've been a number of
things but I would never know until I showed up. I said goodbye to my family and the place I once called home. The vacation was over and it was time to head back to my new home.

CHAPTER 21

On my way back to Tucson it seemed the closer I got the more anxious I became to know what was going on. We retrieved our luggage and loaded up the Lexus in the airport parking lot. I knew I should've dropped Chocolate off first but I had to see what was going on, I couldn't wait another minute. I pulled up to Studder's block and to my surprise it wasn't a body out, not one Nigga$ in sight. "What the fuck is this!" I spoke out loud and Chocolate heard me. I was usually ice cold when it came to my business; I never gave her an emotion to untangle. But ever since I got Studder's call she knew something was wrong and her set mission was bent on try'n to read me. I pulled up to JBangs, Hawks and Vamps blocks and got the same results. It was a ghost town. The first thing that came to mind was Ricky Slick but to be sure I needed to know what was up with my Nigga$. Chocolate had to get dropped off now so I took her to my Mom's and bounced. I chirped Hawk, "What's good my Nigga$?"

"What's up where you at?"

"Shit! Where I'm at, where you at Hawk? My Nigga$ are you serious right now? I just slid down yo block and it looked like a ghost town."

"Oh! Since you've already been on the block then you should know it's bad. I'm on South Park at Vamp's Grannie's house."

"Alright I'll be there in 10 minutes."

"Alright my Nigga$."

With that I hung up and thought to myself what the fuck was that about. Hawk's tone said a lot but he told me really nothing so I chirped Studder while I headed to South Park.

"What up my Nigga$ where you at?"

"Where I'm at! Shit I'm in traffic."

"Oh yeah! Well pull up on me at Vamp's Grannies. I just talked to Hawk right now they over there."

"Then we on our way and will be there in a minute." "Hey you with JBang?"

"Yeah he riding." With that I hung up and looked at my phone shaking my head; thinking I only been gone two weeks and everybody sounded fucked up. When I pulled up Vamp and Hawk was in his Grannie's front yard. I could tell they were in a heated conversation because Vamp expresses himself with his hands and he couldn't keep them still. I hopped out the Lexus and asked "What's good wit my Nigga$?" Vamp turned all his energy towards me. "Ain't shit good Nigga$, these niggas pulled some hoe ass shit my Nigga$; got shit all fucked up."

"What you talk'n bout? Calm down, calm down, calm down Nigga$ and tell me."

"I'm talking about yo man Nigga$, muthafucken JBang, JBang and Studder shit."

"Wait, wait, wait hold up; what happened my Nigga$, slow down you ain't saying shit."

"Look Nigga$ we was all on the block; Studder's block this weekend. Females and Nigga$ shootin dice, all the shit going on. This Nigga$ Hawk cracking on JBang in the dice game. I guess he feeling salty because he flip the script and got on some high power shit, really disrespectful. Hawk just said fuck it and slid him right there. The Nigga$ was drunk as fuck talk'n bout he go kill Hawk and whoever else want it, so I tell Studder to get that Nigga$ outta here."

"Studder?"

"Yeah."

"Shit that's who called me and told me something was up."

"Man fuck him too Scrap!

Listen my Nigga$ these Nigga$ pull off the block; we think nothing of it until the next day and we're getting ready to get back working only to find out these Nigga$ done hit us both. We both had about half a bird left so that's a whole chicken plus whatever they had left from whatever you left them."

I stood there taking in all what Vamp was saying, like I couldn't believe this shit right here. How could so much change in two weeks and then my thoughts were interrupted when I heard the sound of tires sliding coming to an abrupt stop. I looked and saw a Chevy Tahoe with all the windows down and a female driver. Then suddenly passengers popped up from the seats one in the front and the other directly behind him. Pop! Pop! Pop! Pop! Pop! Pop! Pop! Pop! Pop! Pop! Pop! It happened so fast all I could do was run and Hawk was right behind me but from the corner of my eye I saw Vamp bounce up and return shots Pop! Pop! Pop! Pop! We had made it to the back of the house and out of the line of fire. I expected to see Vamp come from around the other side but all I heard was the Tahoe peel off into the neighborhood. Runnin back to the front Hawk and I shouted "Vamp! Vamp! You good my Nigga$?" The front door swung open and Vamp's Grannie rushed out as fast as she could move, she stumbled then dropped to her knees to hold what was left of her grandson. She rocked him back and forth speaking in the language only mothers and grandmothers knew. Vamp was gone; gunned down by two niggas he called his brothers weeks before and they used me to get him. When the ambulance showed up the police was right there with them and we told the same lies, we don't know who it was, never saw anything, don't have a clue about who would do this. That was the code and even though we happen to be on this side of the barrel we had to stick to it and play it how it goes. Watching Vamps Grannie rock him and kiss him goodbye would be enough for any man to raise hell but when everybody was gone we knew exactly why Vamp was the way he was because all she did was look at me and Hawk in the eyes and say "now go get them muthafuckas."

In two weeks I had lost my Young Nigga$ Vamp, 4 kilos and public enemy #1 and #2 JBang and Studder. They were ahead for the time being but they wouldn't be selling any of that work in the neighborhood. Hawk was my only general and he made it clear that JBang and Studder committed treason and if you were seen with them expect the same treatment they'll receive. We literally hunted every night but those niggas was lying lower than worm sperm. I bought an old beat up Ford Taurus with a monster motor that re-minded me of Rocks. Chocolate drove the Lexus.

It was a couple of months after Vamps funeral I was in traffic with Hawk when Chocolate called me frantic, she was breathing hard and damn near hysterical. "Baby what's wrong, calm down."

"I just saw JBang and Studder."

"What! Where at?"

"On 22nd and Craycroft, I was at the Shell getting gas and they slid up on me daddy."

"What happened, calm down and breathe baby?"

"Punk ass JBang was talking shit; they thought you was in the car and after they saw I was by myself he said. You need to fuck with a real nigga that nigga ain't no boss."

"I was like fuck you nigga and he laughed saying he was going to beat my ass so I reached on him daddy."

"What!

"I shot that nigga daddy. I left so fast I pulled the pump out the socket and drugged it all the way home."

"Did you hit him baby?"

"I don't know, I think so; I shot twice and he stopped and grabbed his face. I think they were chasing me but they turned off."

"Where are you?"

"I'm sitting in the car in the garage."

"Baby go in the house. I'm on my way over there right now."

"Ok daddy."

"Oh yeah what kind of car are they in?"

"A black beamer."

"Alright!"

With that I hung up and headed towards the house. "Aye my Nigga$."

"What's good?"

"That was Chocolate right there, she talking bout JBang and Studder pulled up on her."

"Is that right?"

"Yeah, she said she think she popped JBang."

"What!"

"Yeah man, I don't know my Nigga$ I'm pulling up on her right now."

Chocolate kept her .25 Caliber on her at all times. She knew I wasn't fucking with JBang or Studder but she didn't know the details. I never thought she would have to use it but I guess it was a blessing that she had it. When I pulled into the garage Hawk pointed out the gas pump hanging off the car. Chocolate heard the garage open and came rushing into my arms as I hopped out the Taurus. "Daddy I was so scared, that nigga was on one; he really looked like he wanted to do something to me."

"Don't trip baby you did good; you alright." Hawk pulled the pump out of the tank while I walked Chocolate back into the house.

"You say they were in a black beamer baby?"

"Yeah daddy! A little sporty coupe with dark tints."
"Alright baby you stay in the house; I'm going to hit a few corners with Hawk and see what's up. If you need me call me and stay off the phone; don't tell anybody shit either."
"Alright!"

With that Hawk and I were back in traffic. We ended up with nothing until a few days later it was buzzing JBang got shot in his mouth leaving him with permanent dimples.

After hearing that a slow smile spread across Hawk's face and he looked at me and said "Chocolate wit the shit my Nigga$."

More months passed with a few sightings of JBang and Studder here and there though never enough to catch up with them. I gotta say they were moving smart, they knew we were looking for them and they only made themselves able to be seen when they wanted to be.

CHAPTER 22

Hawk was on the block 24/7. The Young Nigga$ was all in formation. The hood was still 100% ours. Even though the loss of Vamp had a few youngsters second guessing if they wanted to be involved in this hood on hood violence; but for the most part we were deep enough to maintain our status.

I spent a lot of time in the office at the Kush Lounge. Diamond was playing her position like a true pro. I had set her up with a crib on the Northside off of River Rd. and she was loving it and me even more. I knew I was loved by few and hated by many. But that just came with handling your business. Diamond claimed she had something important to tell me as we slid into an ice blue S-Class Benz, white leather seats and sitting on chrome 22's. Diamond found this through a customer that frequented the club and was trying to offer it up to get out of legal problems so I snatched it up. We were out for a night on the town and Diamond looked like a million dollars in motion. She wasn't just fine she was beautiful; more beautiful than anyone I had ever seen and with sex appeal to match. She wore an orange cocktail dress made by Chanel that illuminated her soft butterscotch skin, 3 inch heels and her brown and blonde streaked hair smooth and resting on her shoulders. Once she was seated in the Benz all I could do was smile and say "oh so you doing it like that tonight?" She knew she was killing that dress plus any competition. "So you're going to make me ride with all the windows down huh?" She gave me a little shoulder shrug like it's your world if that's what you wanna do, do it." We pulled off in traffic headed to grab my usual package from the drive thru liquor store on 22nd. I cracked open my bottle of Remy and took a swallow then passed the bottle to Diamond. I lit my backwood and cracked the moon roof catching a glimpse of the stars shining like ice blue diamonds bouncing off the Mercedes. I tried to pass the blunt to Diamond but she refused it and so now she had my attention as I made the left onto Craycroft she was still holding the bottle untouched with the cap back on. "What's up with you Ma?" "Nothing Daddy, why you asking?"

"Shit! You ain't drinking; you ain't smoking what's up?" "Nah I'm just chillin."

"Oh don't tell me you squared up on me."

"C'mon now, you know better, neva that." She smiled and had a glow like no other. I crossed Broadway and asked "so what is it then?" Diamond leaned forward to adjust the music down so I could hear everything she had to say. My first reaction was to slap her hand but she pulled her hand back too fast. "Nah for real daddy I gotta tell you something." I ashed the blunt as I wheeled up to a red light at 5th. Diamond had my full attention; she sat up placing her back against the passenger door looking directly into my eyes while I puffed out clouds and blew them to the stars. I could see the cross traffic light changing and me being the only car at the intersection. She continued as I eased off the break slightly; "Daddy I wanted to let you know I'm Pop! Pop! Pop! Pop! Pop! Pop! Pop! Pop! Pop! Pop! Pop! Glass shattered the rear and passenger windows of the Mercedes. I punched the gas and ducked Pop! Pop! Pop! Pop! Pop! Pop! More shots catch the rear of the S Class. "Baby you alright?" I asked. Diamond was breathing heavy not saying a word until she said. "I'm pregnant!" then ran out of breath as I pulled into Tucson Medical Center which was only a few blocks away but I knew it was too late. All that glow she had vanished as she said her last words with her eyes glued to mine. I watched as the doctors and nurses laid Diamond's lifeless body onto the gurney and attempted to resuscitate as they wheeled her in. "A nurse stated Sir we're going to need you to answer a few questions." I looked at the shot up Mercedes that had two flat tires along with twenty eight bullet holes all along the body and interior; my eyes focused back on the nurse like where could I possibly go. When Tucson police pulled up I was in front of the emergency entrance smoking a Newport. Williams hopped out of his Crown Vic steaming. "Cuff this little bastard, I'm taking him in. Mercedes fucking benz Corey! I guess I've been missing a few parts of the story. Tell me this, how many innocents are going to have to die for the price of your head, you little shit?" I looked at Williams as the patrol officer cuffed me and he sensed I was in no mood for his shit. In the back of my mind I replayed the events of the night as I sat in back of the patrol car then I remembered catching a glimpse of the shooter. How could I slip so hard? After all the shit I had already been through, JBang and Studder were the main priority after Vamp but they weren't our only enemies. Ricky Slick patiently waited to make his move and Face was doing all the dirty work once again. 28 rounds and I wasn't even grazed but Diamond lost her life. This shit made me sick… all of it.

I was taken downtown where I stuck to the code of the streets once again. The Mercedes was taken to the police impound under investigation and when the incident hit the news the whole town knew Diamond was dead and she was with me. They showed my shot up Benz under the emergency room sign at TMC on the breaking news alert. When Chocolate picked me up at the station she already knew the story. I hopped in her Lexus and we rode in complete silence. Diamond's blood stained my clothes; I guess Chocolate knew if she didn't want to hear no lies she wouldn't ask no questions. The silence was cold as a New York winter; I believe Chocolate sensed it was something between me and Diamond she would never understand so she kept whatever she was feeling to herself. I was caught up in my own emotions and paid no attention to anybody else's.

The autopsy confirmed that Diamond was pregnant. I was officially on another level. Hawk had tried to get in touch with me for weeks and Chocolate and I were awkwardly silent in our moments together. I had pushed everyone away because no one really knew what I and Diamond had. I kept her to the side like she was supposed to be. Hawk didn't even know about her. I had to eat all this by myself; so right in my V.I.P. booth at the Kush Lounge is where I was spending most of my time throwing back shot after shot until I was interrupted by a Hispanic man demanding to know where Flaco was. I sat back real calm and cool because I could see from his body language and vibe he had something to get off his chest with Flaco. "Aye man, I don't know where Flaco is and he ain't over here, so can you please step out my booth." I guess he took me for a lightweight because he stepped forward, grabbed my bottle of Patron and poured him a shot into an empty glass, took a swallow and said "I know you can get a hold of Flaco saying all this in one motion of pouring himself another shot; a thought came to me that this nigga is crazy. Confirming that he says "Here's what I want you to do. Tell Flaco if he doesn't have my money by Monday then not to worry about it because I'm going to shut everything down." He raised the shot to his lips and took another swallow then slammed the glass on the table. "Tell him I'm going to start with this little club he has que no." Instinctively my hand wrapped itself around the Rose` bottle that sat on the table with the Patron and as I rose up I cracked this fool in his head shattering the bottle. The table flipped and the Mexican buckled to the floor. He had blatantly disrespected me only to find himself looking up the barrel of my 40.caliber Smith & Wesson. I struck him again as he pleaded. Now for some reason that really aggravated me to the point I think I blacked out nearly beating him to death. My club security pulled me off him and escorted me to the office where I pulled myself together and called Flaco. "Man Flaco what's up? I just got into it with some of your people."

"Oh yeah! Who Scrap?"

"I don't know, some Pisa came up in here talking about what you owe him and if he isn't paid by Monday he's gonna shut shit down starting with the Kush lounge."

"Don't worry about it Scrap, you did what you had to do right?"

"Right!"

"Ok then, I wanted to talk to you anyway."

"About what?"

"I'm ready to sell you the club in full if you wanna purchase it?"

"What you mean what kind of numbers are you talking about?"

"Don't worry it's not going to set you back too far. We'll meet up and talk soon Scrap."

With that, I hung up the phone and sat behind the desk thinking this could be all mine. I had no idea the Mexican I had just pistol whipped happened to be someone from the Cartel that Flaco answered to. Recently a large shipment came up missing; Flaco claimed it never showed up and all hell was breaking loose. We did the numbers for the club and Flaco had his team with him now flanking him like he was the President of the United States. He introduced me to Primo who he said was his cousin; he said Primo would be handling all of our business from the drug aspect of it. He had a new pep in his step. Flaco had robbed the Cartel for their whole shipment and was starting his own operation from this side of the Border. He cashed out all his investments, restaurants, clothing stores, the club and was now on the untouchable level with money to burn.

Everything was good for about three months, the blocks were pumping and the club was bumping. It was back to stacking; JBang, Studder and Ricky Slick and his squad had ghosted up nowhere to be found. Chocolate was back to her usual self. She was happy because I suggested she get out of the club and open a hair salon with her mom. She was excited about the idea and really into finding a space to lease. Turned out that Primo was a little more difficult to work with, he barely spoke English and although Flaco had told him about our relationship we still had to establish ours. He really didn't give a damn how tight me and Flaco were.

Everything changed when the car phone rang to my 745 BMW.

"Aye my Nigga$!"

"What's up with it Hawk?"

"Bra I've been out here all morning it's a van on the block in front of Lisa's looking real outta place Bra. I had Big Hic check them out and he said "yeah fa sho bra they're taking flicks of the spot and jack'n folks up when they get down the street."

"They still there my Nigga$?"

"Yeah bra right now."

"Alright my Nigga$ I'll be there to swoop you up in a minute I have to stop by the club first then I'm on my way." I hung up and headed to the Kush Lounge but as I pulled into the Warehouse District the police had the street to the club blocked off. I could see that the club had been hit from a distance and kept driving. I called the club and instead of Candy the bartender answering the husky voice of a man answered. "Who is this? I asked."

"This is the Federal Bureau of Investigations." I paused a split second in denial then hung up the phone. I hopped on the freeway heading south then dialed Flacos number; it took 5 calls for him to answer. "Que onda Scrap?

"Damn man! You got me blowing you up where you at?"

"I had to get out of town, I caught some heat."

"Tell me about it, it seems it's all on me now, the Feds hit the club and they got a van on one of my blocks taking pictures."

"That's not good Que no, you better lay low. Remember I told you it's a time to play and a time to lay. Compa right now it's a time to lay. I don't know my friend but I suggest you cut all ties and get outta there fast." With that I called Chocolate and told her to pack a couple of bags for both of us and that I would be there to get her after I picked up Hawk. I cut the 745 BMW in and out of lanes heading south. When I pulled into Western Hills and down Hawks block I realized I was too late. Unmarked government vehicles polluted the block. I eased down it slowly with only the limo tints protecting me. I watched the Federal agents walking Hawk out of the house with his hands cuffed behind his back; when he noticed me he slightly shook his head letting me know it was all bad. I made my way to the crib, cleared the safe and loaded the bags Chocolate had packed.

"What's wrong daddy, where's Hawk at?"

"I just replied, is this everything?"

"Yeah everything you said to pack is in there, what's going on?"

"Just get in the car and let's go." My destination was unknown, I couldn't call my Mom at this point to tell her what was going on or where I'd be and don't call me to pray either because I was sure all known contact phones were bugged. I felt a little funny because I really needed my Mama to pray for me right now; it was a moment that I thought about God not being interested in anything I had to say because of all the shit that has gone down; but I needed Him to feel me cause something in my spirit just didn't feel right anymore.

CHAPTER 23

I was on the I-10 heading west and 150 miles later I pulled into a resort hotel in North Scottsdale Arizona. Chocolate checked us into a suite after we unloaded our bags and settled in. All I could think about was Hawk and how did all this happen. I was losing everything at once. All that I had worked for was being taken right before my eyes and I had no answers to why.

I had Chocolate call the County jail to see if Hawk was booked in. She came up with nothing until she called the Federal courts only to find Hawk was being held on conspiracy charges and would have a hearing within the next week. I didn't know much but I knew Hawk was able to get rid of what he had in the house before they hit. After about a week at the resort I had to get back to town. I had to retain Hawk a lawyer before his next court date. I was hoping for a bond to be set but the Feds denied all release attempts leaving Hawk to fight his case from the yard. As I pulled on the block all I saw were a group of Young Nigga$ trying to hold it down. I spotted one of the youngsters we had given the monica "ill fetti" and called him to the whip. "Get in my Nigga$, hit a corner with me." He told the rest of the Young Nigga$ he'd be getting with them and we pulled off. ill fetti was one of Hawks Young Nigga$ who had the hustle from the beginning. He would wear the same clothes for weeks at a time; then he'd hit the Mall, buy a new fit and do it again. All he was focused on was the money and that's how he got the name ill fetti.

"Where you been big homie its bad right now, we need some work."

"I know my Nigga$, I got you. From now on you will be supplying the Young Nigga$ and I'll be supplying you. Don't give my line out to nobody, you're the only one who will have this number. Get your money and have mine on time."

"You already know big homie."

"Hawk is down fighting his case so you gotta keep your Nigga$ in line out there. If you don't, it's bound to all go bad." ill fetti sat reclined in the beamer shaking his head in agreement to my every word. I knew he was ready and after we turned a few corners I dropped him back off with a pack and a mission to keep the block pumping. I had to stay ahead of the curve because I knew Ricky Slick was watching even though I couldn't see him.

My next move was to invest into a legit business. I knew I would be missing the money from the Kush Lounge being shut down so I had to take what I learned from Flaco and put it to use on my own. First move I made was to have Chocolate and her Mom looking for a spot to open a hair salon. Her Mom was known for doing everybody's hair right out of her own kitchen; all she needed was a little motivation to take it to the next level. It wasn't long before they found the spot and their credit score was high enough to lease the building space. I put up the down payment and 60 days later Robin's Salon was having its Grand Opening. The salon was a full service experience; if you had a desire to pamper yourself this was the place to be. It was classy with its lighting, mirrors, cucumber water and Mimosa's flowing with surround sound smooth jazz playing while the ladies and gentlemen relaxed their minds for a while.

The back office was mine; that's where I would make my drops to ill fetti. I stayed out of site because the building had a back door so I never had to be seen; I could come and go as I please unnoticed.

Hawks absence in the hood brought a new wave of confidence to Ricky Slick. He knew I was out of sight and he knew Vamp was dead and he knew the situation with JBang and Studder. So all he saw was his opportunity to get back what he felt was his. When ill Fetti popped up to the salon I could see it in his face that something wasn't right. "What's good young homie?"

"Awe it ain't shit we can't fix."

"You know that's what I like to hear.

"Everybody eatin?"

"Yeah big homie I just wanted to let you know in person that Ricky Slick and Face been pushing through the hood heavy; you know since all the Young Nigga$ on one block it's a lot of open real estate."

"As long as they ain't slide'n up like they try'n to get comfortable; stay watchful cause ain't no telling."

"Alright! I want y'all to post up and get money, don't even sweat them unless they get disrespectful; other than that just keep doing what you do."

"Alright big bro." I handed ill Fetti his pack and he was off. I knew this was coming and I was trying to be ready for it when it came; but the fact is I wasn't ready for another war. Wars were expensive and the salon profits were nothing like the Kush Lounge. I had an important meeting set up with Hawks lawyer who always had his hand out for more money. Another ten thousand would get Hawk a 5 year deal on conspiracy charges which he continuously explained to me that that was a blessing alone when it came to dealing with the Feds. It pissed me off because I knew they never caught Hawk with anything; all they had was a witness who made a statement which gave them more than enough reason to slap the clamps on you. After I paid the lawyer his last payment he handed me a manila envelope and said. "Hakeem said you would want to see this." We shook hands and I made my way out of his office. When I made my way to the Beamer I hopped in and opened the envelope and pulled out the highlighted transcripts. It didn't take long for me to see that the witness the FED's had was Primo; and that he had got caught up and rolled on Flaco which had brought the heat to us. Hawk was about to sign a deal for 5 because of some third party shit. I had just copped a large pack from this muthafucka. He was playing both sides of the game at our expense. Flaco was nowhere to be found but Primo was. He had crossed the line and had burnt the bridge that Flaco and I built. I had something for his ass but first I would have to get my Young Nigga$ together.

JBang and Studder had exhausted all their spots; they weren't welcome. Nobody wanted the trouble that followed them to pop up on their front porch. So JBang came up with a plan to join up with Ricky Slick since they shared the same enemy. Studder wasn't totally convinced that it was the best move; he knew Ricky Slick wasn't to be trusted. "What else are we going to do Studder?" JBang asked. You know how it go, if we share enemies you're a friend to me."

"Bra I hear you but it's a dangerous game you're playing."

"Man fuck all that, we need to get Scrap out the way so we can get back in the hood; now is you with me or not cause I'm finna set it up?"

"Damn bra you already know I got you."

"Then stop acting like we ain't rid'n til the tires pop and brakes lock."

The meeting was set in a public establishment but it really didn't matter because everyone attending was crazy enough to shoot it out right there in broad daylight. Face and Dog sat on both sides of Ricky Slick in the corner of Pappadeaux Restaurant cracking crab legs and eating shrimp. When JBang and Studder sat down to join them Face contained his murderous feelings under an instruction of Ricky Slick who simply said if they ain't talking bout nothing they're dead." As soon as they were seated they placed an order with the waitress and as soon as she walked away Ricky Slick kicked into gear as the leader of the conversation saying "so here we all are Bang whats it go be?" He had a little more arrogance than usual that JBang and Studder picked up on and they thought they were ready for whatever they had to deal with so JBang launched his plan. "The way I see it is simple Ricky Slick, we squash all this between each other and get the hood back to what its supposed to be. Scrap is the only nigga eating right now and he ain't fuckin wit none of us; so if we share the same common problem why is it that we ain't partners so we can get rid of the problem." This tickled Ricky Slick to the point he couldn't even hold it in. "So let me get this straight, you saying you want to be partners with me because we share the same enemy?"

"That's exactly what I'm saying." Ricky Slick shook his head in agreement as he began wrapping JBangs angle around in his mind.

"You know that's not a bad idea but enlighten me on how you plan to solve all our past issues and the main one we obviously share." Studder was uneasy as soon as the past was brought up. He sat with the Mac 11 on his waist and was tempted to rise and wet up the table but JBang looked away from him and continued feeding Ricky Slicks ego; something we all knew he found hard to resist. "What do you want me to do to put the past to rest and move forward with what I'm talking about?" Ricky Slick dipped his crab meat into the bowl of melted butter on the table. JBang watched as he lifted the meat to his mouth, butter dripped and slid down the side of his mouth. He grabbed a handkerchief to wipe his hands but neglected to wipe his mouth and simply said "kill Scrap." Bang thought this nasty eatin slick ass nigga got his name from food dripping down his face. When we were finished all sides shook hands in agreement and everything would be squashed between them as long as JBang and Studder help up their side of the deal. As soon as Slick was in the comfort of his big body Benz he stated to Face and Dog. "Them niggas is as shady as they come; watch them closer than what your eyes allow."

I pulled into the hood to check up on Fetti and to bring him up to speed on my next move. It was time to take this operation to the next level and after it was disclosed Fetti had five other Young Nigga$ to bring to the table who were capable. I told them in 3 days we all are going to be sitting on something lovely as long as we handle our business. The deal was set for Primo to bring 50 bricks to a house in the hood that was recently vacant. I had never purchased an order of this amount so I expected Primo to have security. One of my down for whateva Young Nigga$ was posted in the living room closet and others strategically placed throughout the house all strapped with AR15's. I knew if it got to ugly nobody would be walking out of this situation. When three F150 trucks pulled up to the house it was go time. I stood in the living room where a duffle bag sat on the table behind me. Primo had six men with him. I had called my plan accurate because I had six Young Nigga$ with me. When Primo walked into the living room he had the look of a man about to get paid on his face. "Que onda Scrap?"

"What's up Primo?" I replied. He looked around in disgust and asked

"Why are we doing business in this abandoned house?"

"What! You don't like my office?" Primo shook his head and spoke a few words in Spanish to his crew and sat the bag he carried on the table next to mine. "Aye, have you talked to Flaco? I've been trying to reach him and come up with nothing."

"Scrap, Flaco is out of reach right now but I will let him know; now can we do business?" Primo was anxious as hell to get out of there with the money. 50 bricks at $9000 a pop put the ticket 50,000 short of a half a million. When I set up the deal I could hear the anticipation through the phone. I knew I had him. I walked behind the table and reached in my bag and said. "Yeah Primo we can do business but answer me this one. "You fucken the Feds!" In an instant the living room was swarmed with Young Nigga$ waving AR's making Primo and his crew lay face down. The element of surprise was a success as ill Fettti popped out of the closet allowing the rest to appear when they heard my statement to Primo. I placed the 40 cal I had pulled out of the duffel on the table as Primo tried to explain. "Scrap! Scrap! Scrap! What the fuck man?"

"Shut the fuck up!" I shouted. The cat is out the bag and you are the fucken rat." I pulled out copies of the paperwork that was highlighted in areas that showed each one of Primo's confessions and placed them in front of each member of his crew. I didn't know if they understood me but I figured they knew enough to read what Primo had did and why this was happening regardless of if they understood or not; Primo was an informant and he had to pay for that. One of the Mexicans realized what was going on and spit on Primo after rapidly speaking in Spanish to the rest on the floor. "Snatch his ass up Fetti." After Fetti tied him to a chair and duct taped his mouth shut I told the rest of his crew that they were free to go. They took the paperwork with them. I believe they respected my decision so much that the coke didn't even come into question; all I said was "you can tell your boss what happened and why there is no tomorrow for Primo." The Young Nigga$ walked them out and they hopped into their trucks and pulled off. Primo sat in the chair sweating like a stuck pig when I pulled the tape off his mouth he instantly pleaded for his life. "Scrap! Scrap! Please Scrap let me explain. The Young Nigga$ had returned watching him as he pleaded on deaf ears. I opened the closet and pulled out a gas container. Primo saw it and hollered loud enough to wake the dead. The Young Nigga$ shook their heads in disgust listening to him pleading for me to not do this to him. I choked Primo as I poured some of the gas down his throat and drenched him entirely with the remaining liquid in the container. I then told Fetti to grab the work and move back. I lit the match and watched the flames attack Primo before the match had even hit the ground; his eyes lit up and he hollered until he couldn't. The flames had brought the house down on top of him and we left... 50 kilos richer.

CHAPTER 24

I was now at Kingpin status. 50 kilos was more like 80 after we put the magic chef on it. I blessed my Young Nigga$ with 10 bricks between the 6 of them so they all ate with no complaints. I had found property in the Foothills of Tucson pass Oro Valley. The property was iron rod gated with an electric access. The house sat back into the Catalina Mountains and had a view that reached downtown. I gold plated a Young Nigga$ logo on the main entrance to put the final touch of success that it needed. The house was laid out like a mini mansion. Word was out that the Young Nigga$ had jacked the Cartel but nobody had a clue where I was. Chocolate no longer stripped; she just worked at the salon full time. This was the time of my life. I was really on my shit working my angles crossing my t's and dotting my i's. I took everything I learned from everyone and incorporated it into my hustle. I felt untouchable with money to blow. I was the King of my world. Hawk was doing his bid, hearing of all the success and anticipating the day he came home. I made sure while he had to do that 5 piece he would want for nothing. We was taught real Nigga$ do real shit. So that was neva a problem, the least I could do.

Slick was furious when he heard we had moved on the Cartel for 50 bricks; all he could do is push up on JBang and Studder.

"What's going on ain't nobody popped up on the news yet?"

"We on it." JBang replied. It's just that Scrap ain't easy to catch up with no more."

"Well who's running his blocks?"

"As far as we can tell it looks like ill fetti. Every time I pass by ill Fetti out there looking like he's in control."

"Well then follow him and let him lead you to Scrap." "Alright we on it".

It didn't take long for JBang and Studder to find what they wanted; after about a week of following Fetti they figured something was up with the salon then they caught Chocolate stepping out front for a smoke break. "Bingo" JBang stated as he spotted Chocolate. "I know that nigga in there. I should walk in and wet him and his bitch." Studder saw that JBang was on the verge of getting reckless. "Just chill my nigga, we go get this nigga and finish it. He don't know we out here so we got all the time in the world." Studder cranked the engine and circled around the back where a 745 BMW was parked by the back door of the salon.

"That's his shit right there Studder!"

"Yeah we got his ass now." They pulled off and came up with a plan for the next time Fetti made his trip to the salon.

It came a week later. I was sitting in the back office of the salon browsing on the computer waiting on Fetti to show up.

Chocolate and her mom were busy with a couple of clients when Fetti arrived to pick up his package. We small talked for a few then he was off back to the hood. It wasn't 10 minutes after he was gone when I heard the sound of glass breaking and a loud scream. "What the fuck!" I jumped up and came to the front of the salon only to see that it was on fire. Someone had thrown Molotov cocktails through the window of the shop. Chocolate, her mom and customers had managed to make it out of the front but I had to go back to the office to clear the safe of the cash and work. I could feel the heat from the front of the salon as I placed the items from the safe into the Gucci duffle. The salon was burning and there was no way I would be able to walk out the front. I opened the back door; stepped out and Pop! Pop! Pop! Pop! Pop! More shots echoed and I knew it was over; I could feel them closing in. Damn! But I would never let myself give up; even though it felt like I was waiting for that fatal shot. I was stuck between a rock and a hard place for real. Pop! Pop! Pop! Pop! Pop! Pop! Then the sound of screeching tires speeding off. My heart raced as I checked to see if I was hit and noticed all the bullet holes in the hoods of some of the parked cars. Some even had shattered windows. After realizing I wasn't hit I picked up my duffel I had dropped, hopped into my beamer and was in the traffic. The paranoid feeling I had because of the attempt on my life had taken over. "Who the fuck was that? Did Fetti just set me up?" I never saw the shooter or who had thrown the cocktail. While I was thinking my car phone rang, it was Chocolate. "Daddy you alright?"

"Yeah I'm good; you see who it was?"

"Yeah I saw his ass baby, it was JBang who threw the cocktail."

"Oh yeah! I said in disbelief."

"Yup he looked right at me and smiled before he threw it; hold up the fire department inspector is about to pull up."

"Aye when them boys start asking you questions you tell them it was an attempt on your boyfriend's life and you don't want to report his status because of fear of more attempts."

"Ok daddy I'll tell them that."

"Use a customer's name to be your boyfriend."

"Alright baby."

"I'll be at the house; and Chocolate, make sure you're not followed before you pull up." I hung up and continued to push the Beamer through town thinking to myself how them niggas find out where I was and it became clear they must've followed Fetti to the shop. "Aye my nigga$ where you at?" I asked calmly through the receiver of my built-in telephone.

"I just got back to the block what's good?"

"It's all bad right now, those niggas JBang and Studder tried to get at me at the shop right after you left."

"What? "What you want to do about it?"

"Just be cool, I'll have Chocolate pull up on you. Just keep it on the low; she'll bring you to the crib and we'll put together the plan feel me."

"Alright I got it."

With that I hung up and made my way to the Foothills. Once I arrived I put the code into the modem inside my car and the gate opened. I parked along the oval driveway and stepped inside the security of my own home. I briefly

thought to myself that someone would be committing sui-
cide if they pulled anything fishy around here, I had guns
stashed all over the house. Monitors that covered every
inch of the property and my dogs roamed freely and were
bitters and seriously nothing to play with. Chocolate didn't
even like getting out the car unless I was outside with her;
it took some time but she eventually got used to them.

After Chocolate had answered all the questions the police had; as she slid through the hood to snatch up Fetti she
called and said "the shop had been completely destroyed
along with half of the business next to it." When I asked
about the reporting of the victim's condition she said that
"the police claimed they couldn't lie to the press but they
would do what they could to help." As I waited for Chocolate
to pull up to the house with Fetti the 5 o'clock local news
came on with the shop fire being its top story.

"Today more violence hits our town. This incident took
place on the East side at a new and upcoming business. The
hair salon Nu Image was attacked by a mirage of Molotov
cocktails and bullets. As you can see Tucson Fire had problems getting to and containing this fire before it spread to
the connecting business. Police are not releasing any information on the victims; but are saying the investigation is
ongoing. If you have any information, the contact number
is 88-CRIME where you can remain anonymous. After the
report I sat back relieved they gave no clues that anyone had
survived. At that moment a new seed was planted.

My plan was going to shake up the whole hood; in fact
it would have to reach outside the perimeters of the hood
to pull off. It would open up a lot of action to my enemies
but it would also bring them all out. When Chocolate pulled

up with Fetti I met them outside and put the dogs in their kennel. "Damn big homie this you? Man, why you never bring me up here? this muthafucka laid out." Pointedly I said. "Well you up here now."

"That's right, that's right."

"Just remember its levels to this shit."

"I feel that big homie." All of us walked inside and sat in the living room. Instantly we went to work on my plan. Chocolate I want you to get 50 Rest in Peace shirts made; when the shirts are done I want you to pull up on Fetti in the hood and pass them out. "You gotta sell this shit baby so bring your A-game."

"Ok Daddy!"

"You following me Fetti?"

"Yeah I got it."

"Good because we only got one shot to pull this off. The news didn't report the status of the victims so all JBang and Studder know is what the streets tell them so it's up to y'all to make this work. This is what's going to happen. There will be a closed casket funeral and say I was burned up in the salon. Chocolate, you'll call South Lawn and set it all up. Tell them you lost a family member in Iraq and his body was never recovered but you would like to place all his memories he left behind in the casket. I'll call my mom and get her set up and out the way." Chocolate said Ok but her facial expression showed she didn't want to take it as far as I was going. She knew it would be up to her if it worked or didn't work. I'm sure she was feeling pressured. "Alright Chocolate that's all you need to hear." Once Chocolate was gone Fetti and I went over the politics of the situation. I needed Fetti to be steps ahead of our events.

"Look my Nigga$ when word gets out that I got knocked, Slick is going to come for the hood."

"Fuck that big homie!"

"Hold up Fetti, listen to me, we already steps ahead of him because we know his next move before he does. We're going to let him do what he does. I just need you to keep your Young Nigga$ in line; ain't nothing going to change we're just letting them have a block or two. He wants to believe he can have the whole hood to himself but as long as you do your part right he'll have to find his own workers."

"Alright big homie I got it; but when its time to air their shit out I got you on that too."

"I hear you blood now you make sure you hold this close to you. I'm dead serious Fetti don't let nobody know, for this to work not even your closest Nigga$ can know. Fuck! I can't even let Hawk know you feel me? This is how we gotta play it." Fetti shook his head in agreement thinking to himself it don't get no realer than this. "Tomorrow is go time; everything will be in motion so have yo game face on when Chocolate pulls up on you."

After Chocolate pulled up on the block and passed out the Rest in Peace shirts the word spread like wildfire. Through the Southside, then through the Eastside and soon after everyone who thought they were someone was asking "Did you hear about Scrap?" Every Young Nigga$ was wearing a T-shirt for Scrap and most was ready to shoot up the whole town. This had Fetti feeling conflicted because he wanted to let his Nigga$ know everything was all good but he couldn't. He just sat with a ill look on his face in his own quietness and thought big homie has his reasons. The funeral was set for a week later, Fetti was having a hard time keeping

Nigga$ in line but he made sure to do it. He was even able to talk my mom down and agree to get on the plane right after the service. I know for a fact that was not an easy task knowing her like I do. The attendance was packed shoulder to shoulder. Chocolate sat in the first row with her Mom; her big brown eyes were hidden behind her Gucci shades not revealing a thing. The casket was closed due to the burns from the fire and nobody asked any questions. Fetti and his Young Nigga$ played pallbearers and security. The most surprising in attendance was Ricky Slick and Face paying their respect. Slick even had the nerve to tell Chocolate "if you need anything please call handing her a card."

When Chocolate came through the door with Fetti that night she said. "I bet not ever have to do that again." She was heated as she stormed past me.

"What's up baby? Why you mad?" I asked as she went upstairs.

"What's up Fetti she pull it off?" "Yeah yeah my Nigga$ she could've got an Oscar, Grammy, or whatever the fuck they called. She had me wondering if she knew you was at the pad chillin."

"Nah, you puttin extra on it now! "

"For real though Blood she did that."

When Chocolate made it back downstairs she filled me in on the Ricky Slick situation, I told her to place his number in the dresser, I knew it would come in handy I just didn't know when. I was officially dead and buried as far as the streets were concerned. The word had got all the way to Hawk who was sitting in the United States Federal Penitentiary. Hawk was fucked up mentally but he would have to get through it. Chocolate kept money on his books but at times I could only assume how he was doing but his time was getting short, slowly but surely.

After the funeral Ricky Slick had one order of business to conquer what he had before; get back what he considered was his. He gave Face the green light and the plan was in motion. JBang and Studder got the churp on the Motorola to meet at a location where they would receive their first package from Slick to take back to the hood and set up shop. "We back on! JBang expressed in excitement to Studder as they waited for Face to pull up. They sat in the abandoned shopping plaza right outside of the Pueblo Garden neighborhood. A Hummer pulled alongside with two men both holding AR15's. When they exited the Hummer, JBang's eyes lit up but nothing like the barrels of the assault rifles. He knew it was too late while Studder tried to take a chance on making it out of the vehicle. He opened the door but the shots attacked his torso before he could make it to his feet; he slumped over straight to the concrete. Flacka, Flacka, Flacka, Flacka, Flacka shots sounded off like a shooting range but this time they practiced with live targets. When the Hummer peeled off Face and Bolo both put new magazines in their weapons. Just in case the police had a problem with what had just happened.

A month after the murders of JBang and Studder, Fetti had the Young Nigga$ in line and the block was active. The only thing that had changed in the Hood was that Ricky Slick had Face and his crew of older homies on Monterey; which was about a block and a half away from Fetti. This was where Slick made his occasional appearances and sometimes getting a little mannish by sliding down Fetti's block. They say history repeats itself so take lessons and learn; then apply it when it comes back around again. I guess Ricky Slick had learned about fuckin with them Young Nigga$ because as much as he hated to see Fetti running his own block he didn't want to turn the Hood into a war zone again. His approach was more civilized and businesslike. He would pull up on Fetti and shop his package and Fetti would simply say "I'm straight." This is what irked him the most and they didn't call him Slick for nothing; so I made sure Fetti kept a close eye on his operation on Monterey. Months passed then years. I had sat in the comfort of my house and ran the hood from a grave. I had grown a beard and dreadlocks and waited on a date to arrive that was finally here. A long road had been traveled while Hawk was away. I had gained much and lost much but at the end of it all I had made it to see my Nigga$ come home from the F.E.D.S. By this time the hood was split, Ricky Slick had two blocks and the Young Nigga$ had two blocks. Fetti and the Young Nigga$ waited patiently to be let off the leash to shut down Slicks whole operation. I told them they would get their chance to bite down but to me it was like playing chess. You couldn't rush a move; everything had to be strategically set up and I was steps ahead in my setup process for the Young Boss who was coming home.

CHAPTER 25

Chocolate pushed the 600 Benz down the long bumpy road to the Federal Prison Complex. Smiling and looking back at me through the rearview mirror as I sipped my Cognac and pulled on my tree I teased her saying "she better watch where she's going." She pulled up to the guard booth that sat on Wilmot Rd. and told the Officer she was there to pick up Hakeem Harris who was getting released. He looked at his clipboard for a second then pointed to where the once inmates but now free men would be dropped off by the department officials. When the van pulled up Hawk was the first to hop out. Chocolate sat on the hood of the Benz so he would see her. She walked to him and they embraced. As they made it back to the Benz Chocolate explained that she told his mom she would pick him up. When I opened the back door and stepped out, Hawk looked at me real long then said. "Is that my Nigga$?" Nah that ain't my Nigga$! What the fuck; awe shit my Nigga$ done pulled a Makaveli on these niggas." Tears of joy fell from his eyes as we embraced. "I thought you was gone my Nigga$, I can't believe this shit. I was just thinking about you."

"It's all Gucci my Nigga$ let's get up outta here before these Feds figure out what's going on."

"I feel that lets go! Hawk replied."

We both hopped in the back seat as Chocolate pulled off. "Yeah my Nigga$ its been real since you've been gone. Young Fetti has been holding down the block keep'n the rest of the Young Nigga$ in "get it" mode; he's proved me right cause I always knew Fetti was a hustla. That nigga Slick is back in the hood and confined to two blocks since I've been dead but Jesus rose up ya feel me?"

"Hell yeah!" Hawk replied.

"But fuck all that' it's your day my Nigga$ we bout to tear the mall down." Chocolate made it to Park Mall located on the East side. It was still early so Hawk wasn't going to have to deal with large crowds in getting what he wanted. I handed him a 10G stack all hundreds. By the time Hawk had hit all the stores we were walking around with bags, bags and more bags. Before we left the shoe store a female asked Hawk for his autograph. When I asked him what he put on it? Hawk said "Young Nigga$." I busted up laughing because that was that original shit I missed from him. Even though it was his day it felt just as much mine.

After leaving the mall Chocolate drove to a local automotive dealer where I had purchased a few of my whips. When we pulled into the lot the first car we noticed was a white on white S-type Jaguar that was ribbon wrapped with a red bow. The lot had some nice foreign whips on it but everything about that Jag screamed custom; it stood out like a stripper with all her clothes on. Hawk's eyes were scanning the lot when I asked "what you think about that Jag?"

"That muthafucka clean bra." Chocolate leaned over the front seat and tossed a set of keys in his lap. "It's already yours my Nigga$."

"Naw! You bullshittin Blood."

"Real talk my Nigga$." Hawk couldn't believe it as he hopped out of the Benz and pressed the unlock button in his hand. The headlights winked and the grin on his face was infectious. He said "that's my muthafuckn Nigga$."

After we loaded Hawk's bags into the Jag we pulled off and headed to the Foothills so Hawk could wash the jail off him and get fresh. Fetti had pulled up to the crib to greet his big homie and looking at Hawk he was ready. All of us hopped in the Jag for a night on the town leaving Chocolate at home. It had been a long while since I had been out but tonight I didn't give a damn, this was a celebration. We hit club after club throwing back shots having a ball. By the time we made it back to the house the sun was cracking the morning sky. Hawk and Fetti had a set of bitches following that I normally wouldn't allow to see my crib but I was so faded and happy that I didn't even sweat it; all I knew was my Nigga$ was home. Hawk and Fetti each found a room with their guests while I climbed my drunk ass in the bed with Chocolate. Before I could close my eyes Chocolate rolled over and looked me in the face and said. "Do you even realize how reckless you were tonight?" She was right and I couldn't deny it. All I needed was someone to recognize me behind the beard and dreads. "You right baby I was slippin." The next phase of my plan had to be flawless and I couldn't risk it all for a good time and that's exactly what I had done…

Having a good female by my side had taken my game to another level. Chocolate had opened my mind to many levels of this deadly game I played. She played for her position really well; well enough that I was planning on using her for my final move against Ricky Slick. When I talked to Hawk about it he thought I should rethink it. "Blood, do you hear what you are saying?" You wanna send Chocolate at Slick; man you gonna fuck around and get her smoked."

"Just hear me out Hawk; Slick gave Chocolate his number at my funeral and said call when you need something. You tell me then how else are we going to draw this nigga out?"

"Shit I was thinking we catch this nigga in traffic and wake his game up."

"Yeah, if it was only that easy." I knew this conversation was not gonna lead me to where I wanted to be so we cut it short. I was set in my ways but Hawk's opinion did matter to me. He was back in the hood, maybe he was seeing something I wasn't. I found myself in conflict with my next decision and the one voice I heard was Rock's words echoing in my head. "Never let these niggas see you coming Scrap." It had got me this far. Why would I change it now?

The more time Hawk and I spent together the more reckless I was becoming; even though in the back of my mind I knew I should be careful. Hawk just brought out a side of me that I had caged up for so long it was like a piece of me was locked up with him and when he got free I got free. We found a set of Asian twins that loved to entertain real Nigga$ and pulled disappearing acts inside the J.W. Marriott at the Starr Pass Resort. Miko and Shoni hung with us for a week; pop'n champagne bottles and feeding us strawberries in the Jacuzzi with a whole lot of freaking going on. I knew

Hawk was living what he felt he had missed but it didn't answer the question in my head; what the hell was I doing? By the time I made it home Chocolate had packed up her things and was gone. I couldn't blame her she had called a million times wondering when I was coming home. I would answer and say the usual "I'll be home in a minute." The straw that broke the camel's back was when she heard Miko and Shani laughing in the background. I knew where she was but there was no way I was going to chase her.

Chocolate sat in her mother's living room thinking to herself "this nigga got me fucked up." She was steamed but she knew this feeling all too well. She wouldn't let it defeat her like she did in the past. She looked through her bags until she came across what she was looking for. She found that little white card with the number she thought would set her up. She grabbed the phone that hung on the wall in the kitchen and dialed the number.

"Hello hello?"

"What's up?"

"I'm calling to speak with Ricky Slick."

"Ricky Slick hunh, who is this?"

"This is Chocolate, I got this number a while back."

"Yeah yeah I remember no need to explain what can I help you with?"

"I don't know why I'm calling. I just came across this card and I remember how nice you were to me, I'm sorry." "Nah don't be sorry it ain't nothing to be sorry about. I'm glad you called; in fact why don't you let me send a driver to pick you up and we have dinner together?" Chocolate paused for a long second then said. "That would be nice." "Ok then! Text me an address and I'll send a driver." Alright just give me a couple of hours to get ready." "Take your time baby, we don't rush for nothing these days." After Chocolate hung up she grabbed an outfit out of her luggage and ran some bathwater and as she soaked her dark chocolate skin in the bubbles she cried until her eyes couldn't produce anymore tears. When her ride arrived she glowed like the light on a porch on a dark block. She was the flame that attracted moths and her walk had a silky movement as her body swayed from left to right in natural rhythm. Looking at her you couldn't tell her heart ached in any way for Scrap. She slid into the backseat of a S550 Mercedes and as the driver pulled off she thought to herself it's too late to turn back now.

Days had passed and I had heard nothing from Chocolate. I had even called over to her mothers who had told me her stuff was there but she hadn't been there in days. I guess she was finally tired of my shit. I had pushed her to the point of getting lost and it seemed wherever she was she didn't want me to find her. She knew where I was and how to reach me if she needed to. At this point I could care less plus I had two Asian freaks that would do whatever to keep my mind off Chocolate. I was breaking my own rules and bringing them up to the house now. I can't lie I was comfortable with Chocolate's absence after a month had passed with no calls or messages from her. I said "fuck it" she must be comfortable too. Nothing could have prepared me for what I would hear next.

After Chocolate's dinner with Ricky Slick there was no need for her to be dropped off at her mothers' house. Slick wasted no time when he wanted something and Chocolate was one he wouldn't allow to slip out of his grasp. Her pedigree was 100% authentic so he pressed her like a full court basketball game until she couldn't deny anything he required of her. She sipped her wine, smiled and agreed by the time the meal was gone Slick had Chocolate leaving all she had behind and starting something new with Slick. That night she fucked him like yesterday didn't exist and tomorrow wasn't promised; then tomorrow came and they went shopping. She got all new top to bottom and left what she had at her mother's. Her old phone was tossed, buried like her past relationship as far as Slick understood it to be. Chocolate knew that was a secret that would have to be kept or she would be buried for real.

Hawk was back in the hood with ill fetti and the rest of the Young Nigga$ getting money. Although Hawk didn't have to post on the block with the rest of the crew he loved to do it. They were posted shooting dice when a black S550 hit the corner. SuWoop was called out and everyone paused and looked into the direction it came from. The rare occasion of the black Mercedes easing its way towards the Young Nigga$ had them clutching as the Mercedes pulled up slowly to the curb. "Y'all be easy" Hawk instructed. When both rear seat windows rolled down Hawk was taken by surprise at first but he held his composure. "Hawk! I meant no disrespect pulling up on your block like this but since we don't share phone lines I figured this is the only way I could get a hold of you. Hawk's next words cut deep. "A hold of me for what nigga?"

"Expansion! Slick actually tripped over his words. You you know I don't see why we can't put our heads together and find a way to expand." Chocolate sat next to Slick all dolled up not even making eye contact with Hawk. She kept her eyes forward as if she was watching a screen on the headrest in front of her. "You know what Slick? I think it would be in your best interest to pull off my block before you find yourself boxed in a situation you and your uh lady can't get out of." In an instant ill fetti and the rest drew down on Slick, Chocolate and his driver. Slick kept cool and rolled his windows up as they pulled off slowly leaving Hawk's block. Chocolate shook her head thinking what did she get herself into? She instantly thought Scrap had never ever put her in a situation like that. It was too late now, she had made her bed.

CHAPTER 26

"That scandalous bitch!" Hawk couldn't contain himself after the Benz pulled off. ill fetti knew exactly what Hawk was referring to, everyone else just wanted to shoot some shit up so they hadn't really noticed. ill fetti asked "whats up big homie what we go do about that?"

"We keep getting this money." Hawk rolled the dice like there was nothing to it but everything was coming down on his head hard. When he finally left the block he took Fetti with him to the Foothills of Tucson to give Scrap the update on Slick and Chocolate situation. Walking through the door Scrap sat at the dining table being served by the twins a steak dinner. "Scrap, we need to talk."

"What's up wit it my Nigga$ y'all hungry?"

"Nah that can wait." Scrap heard Hawks' tone in that statement and knew instinctively that the conversation that was coming was one that he probably wasn't going to like. He instructed the twins to go upstairs and when they were out of sight Hawk and Fetti joined Scrap at the table. "Blood tell me you didn't do what I think you did?" Hawk asked.

Puzzled by the question, Scrap only could ask one. "Tell me what you think I did and I'll tell you if I did it or not."

"Remember that thing you was talk'n about; you know sending Chocolate." Scrap paused for a second, "yeah yeah I remember. You're talking about sending her to ole boy right?" Hawk shook his head in agreement.

"Nah man, you know after we talked about it I decided to go another route."

"Damn! Then we got some serious problems."

"Why you saying that?"

"I saw Chocolate today; she pulled up on the block sitting in the back seat with Slick in his Benz. She wouldn't even make eye contact with me." My telltale reply that you've got my full attention "Is that right slipped right out? The bitch is sleeping with the enemy and he fronted her by pulling up on the block with her."

"So think about it Scrap" Hawk interrupted. It's only a matter of time before she lets him know you're still alive." "Nah we ain't got to worry about that; if she tells him that he will never trust her again. He only showed up to let you know where she was and he had her."

"Yeah but we can't take any chances. What's our next move? Those niggas are too close for all the tension that's building up. We had to draw down on that nigga to get him to pull off." Scrap paused in thought thinking about how Chocolate crossed all lines. "We'll put something together for all them niggas; just give me a minute to get my head wrapped around this then I'll get back with y'all." Hawk and Fetti both said "take your time" and then walked out leaving Scrap where they found him. When they hopped into the

Jag, Fetti simply asked "do you think the homie is in the right frame of mind?"

"I don't know my Nigga$, I really don't know."

It took me about a month to put my next move together. I knew we wasn't going to make no money in another full fledged war with Ricky Slick but I felt I had to resurface so he would understand everything is not what it seems. I knew this would shake Slick up and it would cause him to keep a close eye on Chocolate. It might even cause him to push on the Young Nigga$ block. After talking with Hawk and Fetti, we all agreed to have a meeting with the rest of the Young Nigga$. In fact this meeting would be a celebration, a celebration of the resurrection and reincarnation of Scrap. The one who everyone thought was gone but not forgotten. After the decision was made I realized Slick wasn't going to be the only one shook. I still had the Feds to watch out for so I had to be careful but it was way past the time for me to surface back in the hood. The meeting was set for the next week and we planned on doing it big.

The more time Chocolate spent with Slick the more she recognized she had made a mistake. She sat around plotting how to make her exit. It wasn't going to be an easy task because Slick kept her escorted by one of his goons. The only time they were alone was when Slick was fucking her and all that did for her was expose his weakness. To her Slick was a tenderdick; once she gave him an unrestricted sample of that brown sugar he was hooked like a big mouth bass. He handed over combinations to the safe, started buying her gifts such as that white ice jewelry she loved. Whenever he wanted to play boss he had to pop up with boss shit. She played her position well and knew even with all the pillow talk Slick did she could end up dead and missing before he just let her walk away. She couldn't believe how Scrap at his young age was so much more advanced mentally than Slick. Now up close and personal she could see how Scrap was able to run circles around these suckers. The more she thought about it the more she missed Scrap. Her mind was made up; she just needed to get out of the situation she was in then she was going back to Scrap. She knew Scrap wouldn't just take her back if she just popped up. The trust line had been broken so she continued to plot until it would all make sense and then it did and she knew what she would have to do to be back with Scrap.

The celebration was set up to be a block party. The city was paid so it could all be legit. We had one end of the street blocked off so it could only be accessed by foot and we had an entertainment stage set up so the local hometown and neighborhood rappers could perform. Barrel grills lined the block with different kinds of Bar-B-Q and sides to go with it. There looked to be over 100 people in the street and it had just begun. I was sure this was going to be the Event of the Year before it was over. The twins chauffeured me through the crowd and parked in a spot that was reserved for me. Hawk, ill Fetti and about 30 of the Young Nigga$ were all in the front yard. Miko hopped out of the drivers' seat and opened my door. I had on my Young Nigga$ fitted cap with it pulled down low over my eyebrows; my dreds hung down to my chest. I had just lit a Backwood before I stepped out. As I stood up the first couple of glances I got was who the fuck is that? Then as I studied the crowd in front of me they did the same as I took my steps toward the gate to the yard. I could see in some of their eyes disbelief of what they saw; a ghost in living flesh. Hawk and ill Fetti watched as I told the short version of why it was necessary for my death to happen. I finished it up with now we all know and it ain't no secret that we aren't hiding from no one. This amped the Young Nigga$ and brought a new light to the celebration. Not one reaction was negative, it was all love and given with understanding. "You ain't got to explain a damn thing to me big homie" was the common reaction. We all grabbed a bottle out of the cooler and ill Fetti raised his and said "this is the celebration of the Original Young Nigga$ to Scrap." Hawk said "we're going to leave Scrap buried and resurrect Scrap Ghost; bottles click as the Young Nigga$ all said "Ghost".

A block away on Monterey they all could smell the Bar-B-Que and hear the music playing. Face, Scoop-D and Mars decided they were going to take a walk up the block of the Young Nigga$. The street was so packed it would be purposeless to try and drive up from the open end of the block. When they made their way to the block Fresh was on stage performing his hit song "they heard about me". This was the Young Nigga$ anthem. Everyone was turnt up to the max. Myself and Hawk with Miko and Shani watched the performance from the porch smoking a blunt when I saw some sort of commotion in the crowd. Redwolf, one of the Young Nigga$ had spotted Mars and Scoop-D and pushed up on them. "What you doing on this block?"

"Doin what I do, don't worry about it." Mars replied. "You niggas better tear up out of here fast."

"We ain't going nowhere." Reaching at his waist but pulling nothing out, Redwolf paused then threw a right cross connecting to Mars' jaw line. He instantly locked up as he was falling back and reached for his weapon. Then pop! pop! pop! causing the crowd to break for the closest exit. All the Young Nigga$ saw was Mars trying to get up with a 9 milimeter and Redwolf was down gripping his hip. Everything had a slow motion calm about it even though the crowd was in a panic. I scanned the crowd and peeped Face partially covered by one of the grills; our gazes locked but the expression on his face was empty and in complete denial of who he saw in his view. He dropped on one knee and came up with his weapon fast. Pop! Pop! Pop! Pop! Pop! Pop! From the porch I made a quick dash into the house with Miko, Shani and Hawk right behind me returning fire Pop! Pop! Pop! Pop! Pop! Pop! The Young Nigga$ had rushed Scoop-D and Mars once they realized Mars's weapon had jammed up. Face knew the alleys were friends in this type of situation and used them to make his way back to his block on Monterey where everyone had heard the shots. He instinctively knew Mars and Scoop wouldn't be making it back to their block. Miko started the Benz and we pulled off. I knew Williams was on his way and at the end of it all it had turned out to be a bloody afternoon. Two innocents were hit, Redwolf was hit and Scoop D and Mars lost their life in the middle of the street. Hawk and ill Fetti both got arrested at the hospital where they took Redwolf. Williams had a grudge against all of us and claimed he was detaining them for questioning; but we all knew he had nothing.

CHAPTER 27

Face pulled up to Ricky Slicks furious. He had looked right into Scrap's eyes. "It was him I ain't trippin" was all he mumbled to himself on the drive to Slicks. Walking in he found Slick in the living room watching the Cardinal's game. "Whats up big shot?" Slick asked.

"It just went down right now, I've been calling you man." Slick brought his chair out of the recline position and turned the TV off so he could hear everything Face had to say. After he looked upwards toward the master bedroom to make sure Chocolate wasn't in sight he asked. "What's up?"

"I just got into a shoot-out with them Young Nigga$. I think Scoop and Mars are dead."

"What happened? Slick calmly asked.

"They had that block party today so we walked over there to check it out and everything went bad.

Chocolate could see from the monitors that they were having a serious conversation so she crept to the door and cracked it to pick up on what was going on that had Slick so focused on what Face was saying. "The worst has yet to come Slick." Face stated.

"What's worse than death Face?"

"Man in the midst of all the commotion I saw Scrap. Man don't look at me like that I'm telling you I saw his face and looked at him directly in his eyes."

"Bullshit!"

"Nah man real shit; the nigga got dreds, they long but its him." Chocolate slowly closed the door and put her back against it. She knew she was out of time and went to the closet safe, punched in the combination and grabbed a 380 taking the safety off as she hurriedly got back into bed and started flipping the pages of a magazine she'd been looking at before all this started. She was trying to calm her nerves because she knew Slick or Face would be coming for her and she had to be ready when they did. "If Scrap is still alive then this bitch!"

"Exactly Slick" Face responded. The rage that was forming in Slick's mind of how he'd been played the whole time Scrap's been dead was enough to turn everything he looked at to stone. He rubbed his beard and said "She don't know we know so you lay low for a minute until everything cools down and then we're going to get this bitch and her nigga for the last time."

"Slick, I don't see why we don't do it now. She knows everything and she knows where he is right now."

"I know she does but he doesn't know where she is cause if he did they would've been done pushed on us. She ain't in contact with him and I'm pretty sure he isn't with her. Oh she'll tell us where he's at, don't worry about that. As a matter of fact Face go to the gas station and get a couple of gallons in that five gallon container that's in the garage. We'll show this bitch when you play with fire you gets burnt."

"That's what I'm talking about." Face walked out to the garage, grabbed the container and hopped in his 96 Impala headed to the gas station.

After Face pulled off Slick no longer had to contain the rage he felt inside. The feeling of embarrassment was something he hadn't felt in a very long time and just under the surface of his rage as he headed up the stairs to the bedroom to look in the face of this treacherous bitch. As Chocolate lay under the covers gripping the 380 Slick walked in saying "what's up baby?"

"Nothing daddy I was about to get up."

"Nah baby you relax I got something for you."

"Oh yeah whats that." Chocolate asked. Slick crawled onto the bed leaning in over her and kissed her passionately on the lips then with anger tweaked her nipple hard causing her to look at him closely because there was no pleasure in it. Slick confirmed her thoughts when he backhanded the shit out of her. "Bitch what the!" Just as fast as his strike, his words were cut off when Chocolate rose up with the 380. Slick relaxed all his tension as Chocolate now stood over him. He knew his only hope was for Face to show up but all his gut was saying is nigga you let a bitch take you out. "You bitch ass nigga." Chocolate shouted at him.

"Baby wait baby look;" was all Slick was able to get out. Bang! Bang! Bang! Bang! Four shots to the face slumped Slick on his own bedspread. All you could hear was Chocolate's heavy breathing; the rest of the house was calm and peace-ful. Chocolate went to the closet safe and cleared it of cash and jewelry placing all items in a Louis Vuitton duffle bag. She knew she had to hurry not knowing who would be pulling up. Slick's body twitched as she was making exit from the bedroom so to make sure there was no life left in him she placed the 380 to his temple and pulled the trigger one more time Bang! The twitch he had left with the rest of his life. Chocolate didn't wait for the 380 to cool off; she put on her Dolce Gabbana shades and made her way to the garage. She hopped in the Mercedes S550, hit the remote to open the door and pulled out to the end of the driveway as Face was turning in. The look he had on his face when he realized it was Chocolate behind the wheel instead of Slick was priceless so she just smiled and waved at him. Face confused drove up to the house ready to express to Slick it was a bad move to let her out of his sight. When he got to the living room he called out to Slick but there was no answer. His heart instantly dropped in his chest as he rushed up the stairs hoping he was wrong. As he opened the master bedroom door and saw his homeboy fucked up all he could say was "That scandalous bitch." Ricky Slick lay in a twisted position dead. Face looked around the room seeing robbery came along with murder. Chocolate had made off with 300 thousand cash dollars and about 250 in jewelry. Hopefully she didn't know about the safe in the garage because there sat enough bricks to literally buy another life; but more importantly those bricks would have opened Scrap's door to let her back in. Face wiped down the house and found the bricks in place. He said words to show his respect as he shut the door to Slicks house and disappeared into traffic. He knew Scrap was still alive and he was going to make sure he payed for everything the Young Nigga$ had coming;

it was just too hot to do anything right now so he did what Slick had wanted and laid low.

Hawk sat cuffed to the table. "C'mon Williams get off the bullshit you ain't got shit on me." Williams laughed and put that shit eat'n grin on his face saying. "What! Do you really think you two are walking up outta here after that shit you pulled today? Nah, my plan is to hold you until I get a witness."

"Man fuck you I ain't got shit to talk about; matter of fact I'm ready to make that call to my lawyer you've been delaying. Chop chop Mr. Williams oh I mean Detective Williams." Williams turned to walk out but not before he said "you think you smarter than Corey don't you? You'll be dead before the year is gone." Williams ordered the officers to let Hawk go in a couple of hours. Fetti sat in Juvenile Hall and would have to stay until Monday to get released.

CHAPTER 28

When Chocolate pulled up to the gate at Scrap's, tears fell from underneath her dark shades. She punched in the code and the gates split open. She pulled the Benz around the circular drive and parked. She grabbed the duffel off the seat and walked up to the door. She was going to ring the bell then thought to turn the knob and see if the door was unlocked and it was. Chocolate thought for once she was not mad at him for not locking the door behind him. Walking in everything was how she had left it. She walked over to the dining room, nobody, then over into the area where we would get our freak on in front of the huge fireplace. Snapping her back to the present was the sound of laughter coming from upstairs.

Miko laid spread eagle and blind folded on the bed as Shani laughed from the bathroom watching Scrap feed her fruits dipped in whip cream. His ass was telling her to guess what kind of fruit it was. "Let me do it, let me do it" Shani asked. Scrap said "go ahead let me see you do it." Shani walked from the bathroom naked looking like a golden

163

goddess. Her hair was pulled up and she moved to a rhythm only she could hear. Miko don't bite this one you have to suck it." She then placed whip cream over her nipple and leaned forward putting the nipple in Miko's mouth. Miko's tongue moved onto the breast slowly; once she made it past the whip cream she smelled Shani's perfume real close to her and her soft moans were turning her on. Her licking became urgent and she wanted to make Shani lose control. She moved to attach herself to Shani's clit but Scrap was already on it. Both of them had accelerated heart rates and looking at Scrap the blood had rushed to his swollen dick making him ready to take it to the next phase of this fiasco.

Chocolate had made her way up the stairs but as she got closer to the bedroom she came across articles of clothing that must have belonged to this naked female laid out by the door of the bedroom. This Nigga$ is really trippin bringing these trick hoes up here. Just outside the bedroom door she heard the moans of Miko and Shani. She went to the vase table in the hall, stuck her hand inside and pulled out a 9 mil Beretta. She dropped the duffle and busted through the doors causing Miko and Shani to scream. Miko pulled her blindfold down to her neck as I looked in shock as Chocolate stood before me with a pistol in her hand staring at me. Our eyes never left each other even when she fired the gun striking Shani 3 times. Paw! Paw! Paw! The shot twisted her causing Miko to scream at the top of her lungs. For some reason no words would form in my mouth, my back was against the headboard as I watched Chocolate raise the Beretta at Miko. "Shut the fuck up bitch." She shouted. Pop! Pop! Pop! 3 more shots struck Miko; all in her torso and the screaming stopped and turned into deep heavy breathing like a last breath being strangled out of someone still trying to fight death. The pain in Chocolate's eye's kept me silent. With no weapon in reach I knew she would pop me if I moved in any direction the stash guns were located; and she knew where they all were.

"Damn Scrap you don't know what I been through. All I asked was for you to keep it real with me and look at all y'all up in here with these bitches like, fuck me. How can you forget someone just like that Scrap? Someone that would kill for you, someone that would die for you, someone that would steal for you." Then she emptied the duffle bag on the bed for me to see the money and jewelry still keeping the weapon on me the whole time. Ricky Slick is dead and I did that for you. I know now you ain't never gonna love me like I love you; yeah I know that now. Pop! Pop! Pop! Pop! Pop! Pop! Pop! Seven shots find my body causing me to slump where I sat. I never thought it would end like this. I swear I didn't see this one coming. My body lay with bullet holes between two bad ass bitches as Chocolate repacked her duffle bag and went over to my safe and punched in the combo and it opened to display the dope, money and jewelry. She had hit two licks and came up. She was now worth a mill ticket and some. This bitch put her shades back on and moved quickly to gather her booty and leave with not even a glance back. She left Slicks S550 and hopped in Scraps Continental GT Coupe. As she pulled out to the gate Hawk was coming through it. He saw Chocolate and she smiled and waved as she left the property. Hawk thought to himself what the fuck was that about. He knew instantly something was wrong because Scrap would not give her keys to a tractor let alone his Continental under no

circumstances. He walked into the house and heard complete silence. Running up the stairs he found Miko, Shani
and Scrap all slumped over on the California King; walking
towards the bed he noticed something and all he could say
was "that scandalous Bitch!"

THE END or is it?

Printed in the United States
by Baker & Taylor Publisher Services